Horse Healer

Eclipse

Nicky pushed his hands deep into his pockets and stayed quiet.

"Now you'd better get out of here," Bretta spat suddenly, "before you upset Eclipse even more." She circled her arms round the horse's neck, leaning against her and stroking her nose. "Come on, girl. It's OK. You'll be all right now."

But it was Nicky Eclipse was watching as he walked away.

And as Nicky reached the gate and sprang across, Eclipse neighed suddenly, a loud, shrill sound that split the night.

It was as if she was calling to him.

Horse Healer
Eclipse

Judy Waite

Hippo

For Nick

Scholastic Children's Books,
Commonwealth House, 1–19 New Oxford Street
London WC1A 1NU, UK
a division of Scholastic Ltd
London ~ New York ~ Toronto ~ Sydney ~ Auckland
Mexico City ~ New Delhi ~ Hong Kong

First published by Scholastic Ltd, 1999

Copyright © Judy Waite, 1999

ISBN 0 439 01007 1

Typeset by
Cambrian Typesetters, Frimley, Camberley, Surrey
Printed by Mackays of Chatham plc

2 4 6 8 10 9 7 5 3 1

The right of Judy Waite to be identified as the author
of this work has been asserted by her in accordance with the
Copyright, Designs and Patents Act, 1988.

Author's Note

While writing this book, I have badgered and bothered lots of people, for lots of information. I am extremely grateful to all of them, and in particular I would like to thank the following:

Monty Roberts – a real-life "horse healer", who inspired me with his warmth and understanding towards horses.

George Summers – the Gypsy Liaison Officer for Hampshire County Council, for his support, time, and information.

The Gypsies of Tynefield Caravan Site, Wickham, and the "Hughes" family, for all their friendliness and hospitality.

Thora Saunders, of Clover Nook Stables, for endless "horsy" reminiscences over cups of tea, and for letting me help out – or just hang around – with her horses.

Becky Littlefield, my riding instructress at Clover Nook, who not only makes sure I keep my heels down and my back straight, but also gives me invaluable background information about the world of horses.

Inspector Stubbington and his colleagues at Fareham Police Station, who even arrested me and locked me up in a cell – all in the name of research, of course!

1

Every time he went, Nicky knew he was doing something wrong. If he ever got caught, he'd really be for it. Except it didn't *feel* wrong. Not in his heart. It was just that he knew that no one else would ever see it in the same way he did.

He slowed his bike to a halt and wheeled it silently into the bushes, wedging it inside a tangle of brambles so it couldn't be seen from the road.

A black car was coming, travelling fast down the country lane. Nicky ducked down out of sight and waited as it roared past.

As the growl of the engine faded into the distance, Nicky straightened up. Stepping softly out into the open, he vaulted lightly across the five-barred gate. He made no sound as he landed.

Quietly, very quietly, he crept between the cluster of trees that lined the edge of the field.

It was dusk, and already shapes and shadows were beginning to spread towards each other across the silence. The moon was out, but its silver crescent was masked behind heavy grey clouds.

In the dusty half-light Nicky could still make out the horse grazing at the far side of the field. Eclipse, an Arab mare, with a coat so dark that in some lights she looked completely black. She had no other markings except for a partial star on her forehead. And she was beautiful. Nicky loved all horses, but she was something above the others. There was a magic about her, a wildness that drew him to her again and again.

He stood for a long time, letting the darkness settle around him, listening to scratchings and scrabblings that rustled the leaves of the whispering trees.

Nearby a twig snapped. Nicky tensed, his sharp green eyes darting towards the sound. It was only a squirrel scuttering up a nearby tree.

Nicky took a deep breath. He felt odd tonight. Jumpy. But he was stupid to feel jumpy. The night would be spoilt if he was on edge. And he didn't want it spoilt. It was too precious. Too special. He was hungry for the buzz of excitement and the racing energy that Eclipse always gave him.

He stepped forward and, low in his throat, he uttered a call. It was a deep, almost animal sound.

Immediately Eclipse lifted her head, her ears flicking forward as she listened.

Nicky called again and Eclipse began to trot towards him, whickering softly.

She drew up close and for a moment they just stood, watching each other. There was no fear between them. Nicky knew Eclipse and Eclipse knew Nicky. He held out his hand and she nuzzled against him. She wasn't looking for treats or tit-bits. Her action was a simple greeting. A warm welcome.

Nicky touched the half-star on her forehead. It was a light movement, very gentle, but Eclipse understood it. It was a sign – a secret message to reassure her, and to strengthen the trust between them. Then he moved to her side. He ran his hand along her neck and shoulder, then leaned against her, catching the rich, sweet smell of her body.

He sprang up on to her.

He didn't kick, or even push with his knees, and although his hands touched the rich silk of her mane, he didn't hold on.

"Walk." He spoke gently, almost whispering, yet Eclipse responded immediately, arching her neck and stepping out proudly as she moved forwards. This was the moment Nicky always loved best, the moving together as if they were almost one animal.

"Now trot." Squeezing with his legs, Nicky guided Eclipse round in a perfect figure of eight, first one way, and then the other. A quiet word made her stop instantly, her nostrils flared and her neck arched. Another squeeze and she was cantering, moving like a dream horse, with a floating grace that had a magic all of its own.

Suddenly Eclipse jumped sideways, rearing up slightly with her ears laid back.

"What the hell do you think you're doing?" A torch beam flashed across Nicky's face. Eclipse snorted and tossed her head.

"Easy. Easy," Nicky murmured. Eclipse stood silent, but her head stayed raised and watchful. She was ready to run if she had to.

Nicky twisted towards the glare, squinting. Even in the darkness he could see the girl. Thin. Scruffy. Shoulder-length brown hair tucked back behind her ears. It couldn't have been worse. It was Bretta Miles, a girl from his class at school.

"Can't you stop waving that torch about? You're frightening the horse."

"*I'm* frightening the horse!" Bretta spoke with an indignant squeal. "Well, I'd love to know what you must be doing, leaping about on her in the dead of night."

"I'm not leaping about. I'm working her quietly."

"But not for long, I bet. You've been here before

haven't you, riding her at night? I've noticed she's been different some mornings. Sweated up and excited. I bet you've been galloping her and everything."

Nicky didn't answer, but Bretta was right. Eclipse had given him some beautiful night rides, racing the moon down the length of the field, or sometimes riding through into the outdoor school where the jumps were always set up.

"You'd better get off, anyway. You're trespassing, and stealing, and all sorts of other things."

For a wild moment, Nicky thought about urging Eclipse on and galloping away. But it wouldn't have done him any good. Bretta would only go running to Edward Carter. Edward was in Nicky's class too. He was friends with Bretta, *and* he owned Eclipse. Between them they wouldn't waste a second before calling the police – or the "gavvers", as Gypsies called them.

A visit from the law was something that Nicky, and the rest of his family, could do without.

He jumped to the ground and Bretta put her hand on the horse's side, walking all round her, checking her legs and hooves with the torch.

"I haven't hurt her. I don't hurt horses. I don't hurt any animals."

"That's not what I've heard."

Nicky stiffened. He knew what Bretta was

5

hinting at. She was talking about the petition the locals had all signed after some newspaper bloke had come sniffing round their site taking photographs. After that people had started complaining because Nicky's family kept their Alsatian dog Sky tied up outside the trailer.

"She's not tied up all the time," Nicky flashed back. "But she's a guard dog. She's got a job to do, and it's what she was trained for. She's probably happier than some sad little lap dog with ribbons in its coat."

"She shouldn't be tied up at all," Bretta retorted. "Animals need to be free."

Once again, Nicky didn't answer. In a way she was right. But they couldn't let Sky loose when they weren't around. She might wander off and get blamed for worrying sheep or something. And they couldn't keep her inside either. Most Gypsies never allowed animals inside their trailers. It would be dirty. Unhygienic. Nicky knew that the gorgios (anyone who didn't have Gypsy blood) didn't seem to worry about things like that, but this probably wasn't a good time to let Bretta Miles know what he thought about house-dwellers' living standards.

His fingers dug suddenly into Eclipse's side, making her flinch and back away in surprise. "Sky's on a long rope," he muttered, "and she can go under the trailer if she's too hot, or if it's wet. We have to keep her there to protect the trailer anyway – to stop people sneaking up and causing trouble for us…"

"A bit like you then. Sneaking out here and riding someone else's horse. That's causing trouble too. If Edward knew you'd been here, riding Eclipse…"

Nicky stared across at Bretta through the darkness. "Does that mean you're not going to tell him?" He hated having to ask. He hated being under Bretta's control like this. But more than that he hated the thought of Edward knowing. Ever since Christmas, when Nicky first started at Maybridge School, Edward never missed an opportunity to jeer or pick on him.

"I ought to tell him." Bretta ran her fingertips over Eclipse, searching for cuts or lumps. "But I'm supposed to be here helping him – looking after Eclipse because Edward can't at the moment. And I really think he's got enough on his plate without worrying that you might be out here, creeping around, don't you?"

Nicky pushed his hands deep into his pockets and stayed quiet.

"Now you'd better get out of here," Bretta spat suddenly, "before you upset Eclipse even more." She circled her arms round the horse's neck, leaning against her and stroking her nose. "Come on, girl. It's OK. You'll be all right now."

7

But it was Nicky Eclipse was watching as he walked away.

And as Nicky reached the gate and sprang across, Eclipse neighed suddenly, a loud, shrill sound that split the night.

It was as if she was calling to him.

2

"Late again?" Miss Bullock raised her huge hairy eyebrows. "That's the third time this term. You know that means detention, and a letter home."

Nicky's tanned skin flushed. Getting a letter home wasn't a problem. Only he and his younger sister Sabrina would have a chance of being able to work out what it said anyway. But detention was a killer. The walls of the classroom already closed in on him by the end of the day. Sometimes, just being in there made him feel physically sick. Even an extra five minutes would be a major torture.

"And tidy yourself up," Miss Bullock's foghorn voice boomed after him as he made his way towards his seat. "You look like you've been attacked by a bag of sawdust."

Snorts and sniggers ran round the classroom, and Nicky flushed again as he tried to brush away the dust and woodshavings that sprinkled his shirt. He'd been out with Dad and Jim since dawn, working to clear a willow tree from somebody's garden. They'd got good money for it, although Nicky always felt a pang at the shudder and crash of those gnarled old beauties that had taken for ever to grow.

He slumped down at the back of the class next to Billy Clarke. There was always a seat spare next to Billy. He was the blacksmith's son, a skinny boy with thick-rimmed glasses and a stammer. Nicky and Billy were often given special lessons together, and before Nicky started at the school it was Billy who had been the butt of all the jokes.

The classroom door opened suddenly, followed by the steady *thwmp, thwmp, thwmp* of rubber tapping the ground. Nicky glanced up as Edward Carter hobbled through on his crutches. He noticed that Miss Bullock's usually sour face seemed to soften. She beamed Edward a huge toothy smile, and she didn't make any spiked remarks about letters or detention to him.

"You got it in the neck a bit earlier, didn't you?"

Nicky turned round, surprised, to find Bretta Miles standing behind him. It was break time, and he always sat round the back of the huts, away from

10

all the shoving and shouting and stupid jeers that were flung his way. Bretta must have followed him over.

"What do you want?" Nicky's green eyes darkened suspiciously. She'd probably come to gripe at him about last night again.

But instead she smiled. "Bullock's always smarmy to Edward. She calls him a 'brave soldier' because he doesn't fuss about his leg." Bretta flicked her wispy fringe away from her eyes. "But I think you've got it rough too, having to work before you come to school. Bullock's a mean old bat, showing you up like that."

Nicky shrugged. "You do it, though. Work in the mornings, I mean. You go over and sort Eclipse out, don't you?"

"That's different. It doesn't feel like work." Bretta walked beside him back towards the school building as the bell went, signalling the end of break. "And anyway, it's only till Edward's leg's better. He's already started riding a bit. His dad wants him to try for the British Junior Show Jumping Team in a few weeks' time. He was training for it last year, but then he had the accident and he couldn't go."

Talking about Edward made Nicky uncomfortable. "About last night," he hesitated. "Are you really going to keep quiet about it?"

"I know you wouldn't hurt Eclipse. I saw the way she looked at you. She wouldn't have done that if you'd ever hurt her. But I was cross, and scared. I mean, galloping her in the dark and stuff is really dangerous."

"It's not, you know." Nicky stopped walking and turned to her. "Horses are a bit like cats. They can see fine in the dark. They're almost nocturnal in the wild. It's because they need to be able to watch for danger at night."

"How do you know that?" Bretta looked at Nicky, interest sparking in her cornflower-blue eyes.

"I've learnt it, I s'pose. From my grandad mainly. He's worked all his life with horses. We both know horses better than people."

"Have you ridden a lot then?"

"My grandad buys and sells horses. I used to help him break the youngsters that he got at the fairs. We'd keep them a few days, then sell them on."

"Only a few days? It takes more than that to break a horse properly."

"It does for the gorgios – that's what we call you house-dwellers – because you try and train the horse to do the things *you* want it to do. We do it another way."

"How?"

Nicky glanced at her. He knew better than to tell a gorgio special Gypsy secrets. Apart from anything

12

else, they didn't usually understand. He kept his voice light. "You just make friends with the horse. Let it know you're on its side. That way it listens to you, and works with you because it wants to, not because it has to."

"It sounds lovely. I can see it might work with some horses, but not all of them. Not the really stroppy ones."

Nicky smiled suddenly, remembering the glow that always raced through him when he got the wildest, most frightened ponies following him around like lambs. "The stroppy ones are the best of all."

"And do you still do it? Help your grandad, I mean."

Nicky's expression closed up suddenly, and he shrugged. "We don't see him any more." He wasn't going to start talking about that either, the stupid fight between Dad and Grandad. Nicky had never known what started it, and Dad would never talk about it. But it was a big enough fight to make them leave their permanent site – Beech Forest – and start travelling on their own. It was just them with their trailer, and Dad's older cousin Jim with his.

And all their real troubles started after that.

"Hey, Bretta! I've been looking for you all break."

Bretta swung round almost guiltily as Edward limped up behind them.

Edward didn't look at Nicky, but he jerked his head in his direction. "He giving you trouble?"

"No." Bretta looked embarrassed. "We were just talking."

"I should keep away from him. You might catch something."

Nicky swung round towards Edward, his fist clenched angrily. "Watch it!"

"That's right. Punch me if you want to. It's easy when you know I can't punch you back." Edward straightened his arms out, leaning forwards on to his crutches.

The two boys eyed each other – Nicky small and wiry, with dark wild hair and restless green eyes; Edward tall and fair, his pale blue eyes always tinged with a mocking stare.

Nicky let his hand drop back to his side, but his face was still tight with anger as he strode away.

3

"What are you doing?"

"Trying to find a square root."

"Then look for a square tree."

"Don't be stupid. It's a maths question." Nicky glared as Sabrina leaned over his shoulder.

"Don't call me stupid!" Sabrina glared back. She tossed her long brown hair defiantly, but her dark eyes filled suddenly with tears. "I get enough of that at school."

"Sorry." Nicky felt hot and irritable. This homework was meant to be in by tomorrow. Miss Bullock had kept him in after lunch, going over it, her voice booming louder and louder each time he got it wrong. When the bell went, Nicky still didn't have a clue about what he was supposed to be doing.

He'd never had to bother much with homework before. If he wasn't out with Grandad and the horses after school, Dad usually needed help with logging and stuff. And the teachers at the other places never used to push him much anyway – they always knew he'd be leaving again, so there wasn't much point.

But Miss Bullock was different. She made Nicky feel like a bit of horse muck when he tried out the usual excuses on her. And Dad was different too – he'd suddenly got this idea that if they were going to survive here, they had to fit in better with the gorgios' ways. Except it was all right for Dad. He wasn't the one stuck doing numbers and writing that tied your head up in knots.

Angrily, Nicky pushed the maths book away and flicked the remote control on the telly. It was children's TV – all cartoons and stuff. Since they'd settled here Nicky and Sabrina seemed to watch more and more telly, but today he couldn't concentrate even on that – the bright chatter and silly voices just annoyed him.

"Can't you stop that?" Sabrina shoved her own homework into her bag, and slumped down between a couple of cushions in front of the screen.

"What?"

"Drumming your fingers on the seat. It's driving me nuts."

16

Nicky pulled a face at her. "I'm going outside. This is just kids' stuff. It's really boring."

Sabrina didn't look round as he slammed out of the door.

Mum was outside, polishing the trailer windows. She jumped, startled, as Nicky came up behind her. "What are you hanging about for?" She glanced over her shoulder at him as she spoke. "If you've nothing to do you could go and give your dad a hand. He's making fences and stuff out of some branches he brought home this afternoon. Jim's there but – " Mum shrugged – "well, let's just say Dad could do with a stronger pair of hands helping him."

"We should have stayed at Beech Forest then. There were plenty of strong hands to help him there. And I don't know why Jim's sticking with us at this dump anyway. It's not as if *he* fell out with anybody."

Mum's face closed suddenly, like it always did when Nicky mentioned Dad's fight with Grandad. She turned her back on him and began rubbing harder, her thin brown hand sweeping across the pane. "Jim got the wanderlust again," she said at last. "He wanted to get back on the road, and it suited him to come with us."

"It suited us to have him too. Who else could Dad get to mind the trailer, or Sabrina, when the rest of us are out?"

Mum sighed. "Don't take it out on Dad all the time. We're all trying to cope in the best way we can. It's not perfect for any of us. None of us would have chosen this."

"Dad chose it," Nicky muttered. But he didn't say it loud enough for Mum to hear. Nicky watched her for a moment. Her dark hair, usually pulled back and braided, swung loose today and hid her face. But he could guess her expression, almost as if he could feel what she was feeling. Her lips would be pursed thin, and her brown eyes heavy and sad. Still, she wouldn't say a word against Dad. She never did.

Nicky pushed his hands deep in his pockets and stared around him. He hated this life: their two trailers parked up on a bit of wasteground with the amenities tip on one side and a huddle of empty garages on the other.

Beech Forest had been so different – set in a quiet clearing hidden by trees, with only a mud track leading up from a country road. It was a permanent site – an official one provided by the council. Different families came and went, travelling between jobs and seasons, but they all knew each other, and got on – most of the time.

And, because Beech Forest was in the heart of the countryside, there were plenty of horses. As well as the buying and selling, Nicky and Grandad went all over the place – working with young horses, fixing up damaged horses, sorting out difficult horses. It wasn't just Gypsies they dealt with. Gorgios trusted them too, and there was always plenty of work.

Beech Forest wasn't the only site they'd ever stayed on, but it was the place they went back to most often in the winter, and it was the one Nicky always loved the best.

"This place is a mess," he said suddenly. "Can't we get rid of all these rotting logs and branches?"

Mum turned on him sharply. "You know Dad doesn't want to risk upsetting the gorgios by dumping it somewhere. They're bound to know it was us."

"You're right there," Nicky's voice tightened. "Even when it isn't us, they say it is."

Nicky looked round at the untidy heaps of wood – stuff from Dad's jobs that he couldn't afford to shift. It seemed stupid, but it cost more to take it to the landfill site than Dad earned from doing the work, and the dump across the road would only take their household rubbish. They said the wood was all "trade waste", and they had to pay to get rid of it. And it was the wrong time of year to bag it up and sell it by the roadside. Thinking about the time of year filled Nicky with a restless ache. Normally, by April, they were getting ready to start travelling again.

He punched the side of the trailer suddenly. "Are we really going to have to live like this for ever?"

Mum's eyes met Nicky's. "You know Dad wants us to settle properly here – to stay in one area permanently."

Nicky looked away, remembering the row between Dad and Grandad that had started all this. He used to sleep in Grandad's trailer then, and he'd been lying awake, his shoulder throbbing from a bite he'd got from a sick horse earlier that day. The poor animal had a brain tumour, and was going mad with the pain.

It was late – gone midnight – when the voices burst out of the silence, shaking the night, probably waking half the site. It was Dad and Grandad. They cursed and shouted for what seemed like hours, and Nicky heard Dad swear they'd never live near Grandad again. He heard the door on Grandad's pick-up slam shut, then it roared away. It didn't come back that night.

They left in the morning, without even waiting to say goodbye to Grandad.

A couple of times Nicky tried to ask Mum and Jim what the row was about, but it was like trying to break a stone with a feather, and in the end he gave up.

The travelling was good at first. It gave them a freedom that Nicky always loved. Some things about it were hard. Finding water. Making money. But that was part of the life, and they were used to it. And if a place didn't work out, if people were rude or rotten to them, it didn't really matter. Not when they could keep moving on.

It was the horses that Nicky missed most. When Grandad was around, horses were around too, but Dad wasn't interested in them. So, as they moved from place to place, Nicky noted where the horses were. Then, once they'd parked up, he slipped back to find them. Whenever he could, he rode – sometimes with the owners' permission, and sometimes without. Dad never knew. If he had, he would probably have stopped it. But Nicky needed to go. He needed to be around horses to keep sane, like some people need the sunshine to keep happy.

In each town or village, Dad and Jim went looking for work.

One day, back in November, they found a builder whose mate had hurt his back, and who needed help to finish repairing some farm buildings. The farmer, who was desperate, agreed to let them pitch up on one of his fields until the job was done.

It was great, staying there. The weather was ice cold, but dry. Nicky and Sabrina made rope swings in the trees, or ran wild across the fields. Although it was winter, Dad wasn't making them go to school, because they weren't planning to be there for long enough.

Then, one day, some of the big detached houses nearby got burgled.

The police came poking around the trailers. They didn't find anything, but that didn't satisfy the locals. They didn't bother to come and see Dad, or Jim. They didn't even talk to the farmer. They just crept up on them in the dead of night.

Nicky heard them first. He always slept in Jim's trailer, and he slept lightly, listening out for sounds of trouble. It was no good relying on Jim. He was almost deaf. He would probably sleep through a herd of elephants dancing on the roof.

So Nicky, awake and restless in bed, heard the soft tread of footsteps crunching across the frosted field. Sky began to bark. He saw the shadows in the trailer change, as thin beams of torchlight danced in through the darkness. He sat up quickly, but it was too late. Bricks were hurled, smashing through the silence, cracking and splitting the windows and smacking all along the side of the trailer. There were shouts, and whoops, and feet stamping like a war dance.

The gang were finished and gone by the time Dad and Nicky, from their different trailers, had run out to face them. Jim didn't even wake up.

The farmer came to see them all next morning, and said he'd "had a phone call, and it would be best if they went on their way."

There was no point arguing. They all knew from experience it never did any good.

So they moved on again.

By the next day they had cleared up the damage – getting new windows, pulling out the knocks and dents, and painting over the vicious graffitti sprayed in violent red all along the outside. But Dad said the real damage was where you couldn't see it. Where you couldn't get at it to mend it properly. It was twisted up deep inside all of them.

And it was true that, since that time, Mum had got thinner and greyer, and there weren't many nights when Nicky didn't hear Sabrina wake up screaming in the trailer next door.

In the end Dad decided enough was enough, and insisted they find a permanent place to settle. This piece of wasteground, on the edge of the small but growing town of Maybridge, was the best they could find. Choosing somewhere grotty, on the rough edge of the town, meant they were less likely to get run off by the gorgios. There was an official Gypsy site ten miles away and they were allowed to get water from there if the petrol stations they usually used got funny, but Pete Dale – the bloke from the council – reckoned they'd have a long wait before he could get them a proper pitch.

But to Nicky's mind, staying here, a small group

in one place, was just as dangerous as being on the farm. People always knew where they were. Night after night they were sitting ducks. If anyone wanted to get at them they could plan it weeks ahead. They could choose their moment. And it might not even be when they were all in, able to stick up for each other. It might happen at a time when one of them was left here on their own.

Suddenly Nicky kicked at a loose stone and walked moodily away from Mum.

He wasn't going over to help Dad and Jim.

He didn't feel like it.

He wandered across to where Sky was lying in a patch of sunlight. As he crouched down beside her she rolled on to her back with her legs in the air, pawing at him to tickle her tummy.

He heard Mum shout, "Nicky! There's somebody here for you!"

He looked up in surprise. Nobody had ever come to see him here before. But across the muddy site a girl was hurrying towards him. It was Bretta.

"Hi." Nicky brushed his dark fringe back from his eyes nervously, wondering if she'd come to tell him she'd changed her mind, and was planning to drop him in it about last night after all.

Whatever it was she seemed breathless and upset. "This was in this evening's paper." Bretta thrust a newspaper clipping at him.

Nicky's face burned. Even a quick glance told him the print was small, and there wasn't any hope he'd be able to read it.

"You can't read what it says, can you? Well, I'll tell you. Although you probably already know."

Still breathless, she began:

EQUINE NIGHTMARE

Another horse has been found paint-sprayed and hobbled in a field just outside Maybridge.

The horse, a grey gelding called "Misty", was discovered early this morning by his owner.

Both the horse's back legs were roped together, and his flanks had been sprayed with an aerosol paint in a pattern that seemed to resemble the letter "Z".

The animal was very frightened, and described by his owner as having been "agitated and confused".

Police are appealing for anyone who saw anything suspicious in that area to come forward.

This is the third incident of its kind since Christmas.

Bretta glared at Nicky. "So where did you go last night, after I caught you riding on Eclipse?"

Nicky was stung. Angry and hurt. "I feel as bad about this as you do. You can't think it was me. You know I don't hurt horses!"

"I don't know anything about you. You could be anyone, and you might do anything. It's a fact you tie dogs up. And you said you know horses better than people. So maybe you know how to put curses on them to get them to come to you."

Nicky's face darkened with anger. Just this morning she'd seemed almost his friend. Now, already, she was turning the things he'd told her back on to him. Gypsy. Tinker. Beggar. Thief. He'd heard it all before. That was what they called him at school, and she wasn't any different from the rest of them. "Believe what you want, then," he scowled. "It's no odds to me."

"It's not just what I believe. It's putting two and two together, to make things make sense. Do you want to know what Edward said about you this morning, after you'd gone?"

"I can't wait."

"He said there was something sneaky about you. That people like you can't ever be trusted."

"And I suppose if your super-hero wonder boy Edward says something, it must be true. You probably haven't got any ideas of your own."

Bretta bristled. "You're wrong. I was actually beginning to like you earlier. I even stuck up for you after you'd gone. But Edward showed me this newspaper when I went over to ride Eclipse just now, and it all suddenly clicked into place. I know you're not supposed to be able to read much, but I expect even you can recognize this…"

Bretta thrust the paper back at him, her finger pointing halfway down the report. "The letter 'Z'. Only Edward said he didn't suppose the poor horse stood still long enough for you to get it perfect. So let's twist the paper a bit. Let's look at it another way."

Bretta's hand was shaking as her finger pointed to the letter, now turned on its side, and which suddenly, even to Nicky, looked clearly like the letter "N".

4

"You resting, lad?" Jim wandered over, dusting his leathered old hands on his baggy grey trousers.

Nicky, sitting hunched against the wheel of the trailer, shrugged. "Just thinking."

"Well, that's a poor bloke's sport. Don't do too much of it. It's dangerous." Jim laughed, then broke off, wheezing suddenly, before heading back to his trailer.

Dad came over. He looked tired, his dark hair wet with sweat, and brown smudges of wood dust down one side of his face. He didn't look at Nicky. He was often like that – as if he couldn't quite look him in the eye. "I've got a job on in a minute. It'll need two of us. Jim's just about had it for today. Will you come?"

"Go on, Nicky. It'll be better than skulking about here all evening with nothing to do." Mum glanced towards him anxiously, then turned back to planting bulbs in the new flower box Dad had just made.

"What sort of job is it?" Nicky scratched a row of numbers into the soft mud with a piece of flint. He should really be back inside, doing that square root stuff, but Bretta's visit was still bugging him. It would be harder than ever to concentrate now.

"Some posh bloke just outside of town. I went and saw him this morning." Dad went over to the pick-up and began clearing out the last of the logs he'd collected earlier. "He's got a load of brick rubble he wants shifting. He's planning to build some new stables, apparently."

Nicky looked up, interested at last. "Sounds OK." He got to his feet, brushing the dust off the seat of his jeans. Anywhere that was near horses had to be better than thinking about numbers fitting into other numbers and ending up being the same as the first number, or whatever it was.

Twenty minutes later he and Dad were rattling through an entrance between two stone pillars with marble horses prancing on the top, and Nicky was cursing quietly to himself.

He might have known it.

He should have checked with Dad exactly where it was they were going.

Nicky had never been through these gates before, but he knew where they were. He'd cycled past here enough times on his way up to the fields. It was Edward Carter's place. He just hoped that neither Edward or Bretta were hanging about.

They drove past the bungalow where Edward lived with his dad – a modern-looking white building with an arched porchway – and stopped near what looked like a converted railway carriage, freshly done up in the same stark white paint. Nicky guessed it was probably accommodation for the stable hand.

Further down the yard, two boys were unsaddling a skittish grey mare, watched over by a tall man in a green leather jacket. Nicky recognized the boys. They were brothers – Liam and Matt Frazer. Matt went to his school, although he was older than Nicky, and in a different year. Nicky suddenly remembered hearing that Matt's older brother worked for Edward's dad.

As Dad cut the engine the man in the green jacket approached them. He was slim and athletic looking, with hard blue eyes in a high-boned face.

"Declan Carter. I own the place." He smiled briefly as he shook Dad's hand. "Good of you to come over at such short notice."

"No problem. Good of you to offer me the chance of some work."

"If you do a decent job there could be more coming up. I'm going to need someone reliable."

"I'm sure you won't have any complaints, will he, Nicky?"

Nicky didn't answer. Pushing his hands deep into his pockets, he dropped behind as they walked down the yard. He hated it when Dad started going all smarmy to the gorgios like that.

There were horses in most of the stables. Class horses, all of them. Nicky could tell it straight away. He stretched his hand out, letting their velvet noses brush against him as he walked past.

"Keep up," Dad called back over his shoulder. "You're dragging."

Dad's look was disapproving, and Nicky knew what it was about. He'd been told often enough. *Don't upset the locals. Don't ever let yourself be seen doing anything that might be called suspicious. Don't give anyone a chance to pin anything on you. If you do, it's like shooting yourself in the foot.*

Nicky was just about to catch up when a familiar whinny sounded from nearby. It was Eclipse, trotting across the field that ran down the opposite length of the stables.

Declan Carter heard her too. He stopped and walked over to the fence. "My son's horse," he said, looking at Nicky for the first time. "She's a star, but a bit hard to handle. My son came off her last year, smashed his leg up a bit. But he's no wimp. He'll be on her again soon. I've got high hopes for them both later this year." Declan Carter's voice had a sharp edge as he leant across to ruffle Eclipse's shining black coat.

Watching him, Nicky had the feeling he was the type of man who was used to getting what he wanted.

As Declan Carter patted her, Eclipse tossed her head and looked past him, snorting at Nicky. Nicky stood back slightly from the fence, hoping Edward's father wouldn't suddenly guess that she recognized him. She'd probably only come over because she'd smelt him. Nicky had known horses to catch the scent of someone they knew from several fields away. In the wild they needed to be able to smell for distant water, and for creeping danger.

"Steady, girl. What's up?" Eclipse continued to ignore Declan Carter as he tried to pull her head round towards him. Eclipse twisted slightly and stretched her neck out to Nicky. She kicked the fence and whinnied loudly, and Nicky felt her puzzlement and frustration because he was hanging back.

"Got a gift with horses, my Nicky." Dad spoke abruptly before turning suddenly away. He didn't sound proud – he sounded angry. Nicky flinched. Dad never praised him for anything he did with horses. Not when he saw him ride. Not when he saw how horses would follow him across a field. Not even when he'd gone out with Grandad and made sick horses better.

Dad had a problem with horses. It was to do with his sister, Ellie, and a terrible riding accident when they were children. Dad never talked about it – he never even mentioned his sister's name. Nicky had only ever managed to pick up scraps of the story from other relatives. But whatever it was that had happened, it was all years and years ago. It never really explained why Dad was still so twisted up about it. All it did was to make a distance between them – a great, dark river that swirled with mistrust and misunderstanding.

"A gift, eh?" Declan Carter whistled softly as he watched Eclipse push harder against the fence. She was still looking past him towards Nicky. Declan Carter raised his eyebrows, but it was impossible to tell if he was annoyed or amused by her obvious preference.

From behind him, Nicky was aware of Liam and Matt watching.

Eclipse whinnied again, trotted in a small, agitated circle, then came back to the fence. As she moved she arched her neck and stretched out her tail, as if she was trying to remind Nicky how beautiful she was. But Nicky didn't need reminding. He felt a sudden twist of jealousy. That jerk Edward Carter had all this...

"We'd better get on." Declan Carter gave Eclipse a last sharp slap on the neck as he turned away. "You'll want to start working before it gets too late."

Eclipse followed them, trotting along the edge of the field until another row of stables blocked her view.

Declan Carter led Dad and Nicky round a corner at the end of the yard. There was a mountain of bricks and planks of wood piled behind the back of an old barn. "It used to be a cow shed, from the days when the place was a farm. But I need more stables up before next winter, so I've got to get it cleared between now and then. There's a couple of barrows by the wall, and you can reverse your pick-up right up to the edge here." He pointed to where a freshly-made road ran alongside a large, expensive-looking double garage. "There's another road joins up round the back. Just drive behind the stables instead of turning right when you get into the yard. Any problems?"

"No. Everything seems fine, doesn't it, Nicky?"

Nicky grunted.

"Good." Declan Carter glanced at his watch. "Now I'll leave you to it. I'm away tonight, and I want to get an early start." He nodded briefly at Dad and strode off.

Nicky worked quickly, side by side with Dad. He was slight, but he was strong, and hard work was no stranger to him. The first pick-up load didn't take them long.

Dad looked at the sky. The light was still good. They probably had at least another hour of working yet. "You get the next barrows loaded up while I drive home to the site with this lot. I'll be back soon."

Nicky nodded, but didn't look round. He had his own reasons for wanting this job over as quickly as possible.

It was hot work, and the evening was warm for April. Nicky took his shirt off and draped it over a fence post. When the barrows were filled, he leaned against the fence, wiping the sweat from his face with the back of his hand.

It was boring, waiting for Dad to reappear. There was a tap on the outside of the garage opposite and, suddenly thirsty, Nicky walked across and cupped his hands underneath to drink the cold, refreshing burst of water.

Then he turned to look at the garage. It looked out of place here, stuck in amongst the old buildings and the muck heap.

Puzzled, Nicky wandered across and peered in through the windows. It was dark inside, but he could make out the shape of something in there. He frowned, rubbing at the glass that was steaming up under his breath. It was a car. A jet black Porsche. Nicky remembered Grandad winning one in some sort of bet at a Gypsy fair one year. He hadn't kept it long. He'd probably gambled it away again, knowing him. But he'd driven Nicky round the field in it and it had given them both a kick, the way everyone turned to watch them, like it was a jewel amongst all the pick-ups and trailers.

Nicky felt really down suddenly. Thinking about Grandad reminded him that they'd miss the big horse fair in two weeks' time. They went every year. All their family did – aunts and uncles and cousins and stuff. Even those that weren't into horses never missed it. But Dad said they couldn't risk leaving the new site this year, or they might come back and find the council – or the locals – had driven posts round it to stop them getting back on. But Nicky knew the fight with Grandad was the real reason. Grandad was bound to be there.

But the throb and colour, the roughness and the horses, were all things Nicky loved. Just being amongst everybody, meeting up with the family, catching up on talk – it all seemed like one big party to him. Even the drunken fights that sometimes woke him at night were part of the buzz of it.

"Do you want something, Gyppo?" Nicky swung round as the voice cut through his thoughts.

Edward Carter was swinging his way towards him on his crutches.

"Nothing that you've got."

"So what are you doing here?"

"Working. I'm with my dad."

Edward raised his eyebrows slightly. "The hired hand, eh? Well, I hope my father's not paying you by the hour."

Nicky didn't answer.

"I suppose you were sussing out the car. Seeing if it was worth creeping back at night for."

"Don't push your luck." Nicky's voice was a growl.

"I don't need to." Edward smiled smoothly. "I know all about you. Much more than you think. I could grind you up with the heel of my boot if I ever wanted to."

Nicky flushed angrily. Bretta Miles! She must have told Edward about him and Eclipse, even though she'd said she wouldn't.

"Pretty though, isn't she. Do you want a closer look?"

Without waiting for a reply, Edward leaned on his crutches, took a remote control handset from his pocket and pressed the switch.

The garage door opened automatically, making a high whining sound as it rose up. At the same time a light flickered on to reveal the car in all its gleam and glory. It was obviously loved and polished. Everything shone, and the chrome sparkled like sunlight. "It's my dad's pride and joy. No one else is allowed near it. Not even his stable hands, Liam and Matt. He lets other people deal with the horses, but he doesn't trust anyone with this." Edward stroked the bonnet lightly, his face alive in a way that Nicky had never seen before.

At that moment there was the rattle of an engine, and Dad's pick-up coughed its way back into the yard.

Edward pressed the remote control switch, the light went off, and the door lowered and closed with that same high whine.

He turned back to Nicky. "Looks like tea break's over." His voice had changed again, and his mouth was twisted in the mocking, familiar sneer.

As Nicky turned and walked back towards the pile of bricks, Edward called after him, "And just remember – if that car ever disappears in the middle of the night, you're going to be top on my list of suspects!"

5

"Heard about those horses last night?" Nicky felt the poke of something hard in his back.

He knew what it was, and he didn't turn round. Edward was allowed to have his chair along the back of the hall in assembly, and this wasn't the first time he'd got himself directly behind Nicky, and given him sly digs with his crutches all the way through.

"I'm talking to you, Gyppo."

This time Nicky half turned. "Leave off, or you'll be sorry."

Edward laughed. "A Gypsy curse perhaps? That should be interesting."

In front of them, other classes were filing in and settling down. There was the usual buzz and clatter of noise, everyone ignoring the barked "Quiet, now!" and "No talking!" warnings from the teachers.

Nicky turned back to face the front of the hall, but the next sharp dig in his back made him spin fully round.

"I'm talking to you, Gyppo. Although I'm probably the only person in the school that will, once they all find out about you."

"There's nothing for them to find out."

"Dad knows the woman who owns those horses. She told him their legs were bleeding from where the friction of the rope burnt into their skin as they tried to get away. It was lucky neither of them broke a leg."

"I didn't do it. Only a nutter would do that to a horse."

"My point exactly, Gyppo. And I don't think my dad's going to be so keen on doling out labouring jobs to your father once he knows what his son's up to."

"Well, he won't find out, because it isn't me, so shut it!"

"Dad says we're going to have to stable Eclipse while this *mystery madman* is still on the prowl. We can't take any chances. We can't have her being mauled about. She's a valuable animal."

"You'll do her harm like that. Horses get vices when they're stuck inside."

"A bit like Gypsies then. Maybe that's what happened to you."

Nicky didn't know if it was the cheap jibe, the threat that Dad might lose the chance of a job, or the sudden flash of Eclipse being stuck in a stable all day that made him do it.

He sprang suddenly to his feet and grabbed Edward by the collar, pulling him up off his chair. The crutches clattered to the floor.

"You're just a jerk, Edward Carter. I bet Eclipse threw you because she couldn't stand you on her back. No horse would choose to carry a prat like you."

Nicky's eyes were dark with anger. Drawing back slightly, he tightened his fist and aimed the first punch.

A couple of girls screamed. A group of boys shouted, "Bundle! Bundle!"

"What is going on?" A furious Miss Bullock was tearing at Nicky and Edward, prising them apart.

"He just went for me, Miss. He's like a wild thing." Edward was spluttering and crying.

Nicky stepped back, but his fist was still clenched.

"Nicky? Is this true?"

The screams and chants had stopped and the hall was silent. The whole school was watching. The whole school was waiting.

Nicky's hands clenched and unclenched, and he wouldn't take his eyes away from Edward's.

Miss Bullock shook him, pinching his shoulder as she gripped him hard. "Nicky Ghiselli, stop this now. You're not doing yourself any favours. You're only making things worse."

He tried to shake her off. She was a big, bulging woman, but she wasn't strong. "Push off, you silly cow." He gave Miss Bullock a fierce shove towards Edward, then, twisting nimbly away, he wriggled free and ran – straight into the path of Mr Nash, the school headmaster.

Mr Nash's room was a muddle. It surprised Nicky to see all the books and files and piles of paper spread about everywhere. Even the phone on his desk was half buried. Nicky wondered if Mr Nash always had to search for it when it rang.

For a moment, he forgot why he was in here, and tried to imagine what Mum would say. It would drive her mad, all this mess. Their trailer was immaculate, with everything in its proper place. Living in a small space made them all like that.

Mr Nash made a dry coughing noise in his throat, and Nicky looked nervously up at him, feeling like a rabbit staring down the barrel of a gun.

For a long time the headmaster stared back with his sad tortoise eyes. He didn't speak.

Uncomfortable, Nicky looked away again.

He gazed out of the window towards the staff car park. It was raining, a dull grey drizzle that had been slipping from the sky all morning. Nicky watched the tiny silver snakes of water that slid down the glass of the window pane. He wished he could be outside, running through the damp day and away from all of this.

"You're not happy here, are you, Nicky?" Mr Nash's voice broke the silence suddenly, making Nicky flinch.

"No."

"It must be hard fitting in. You come from a very different background from all the others."

"I hate it here."

Mr Nash sighed, locking his fingers together on the desk and studying them for a moment. "You do need to have some form of schooling. It's the law."

Nicky knew all about the law. If he and Sabrina didn't go to school for a certain number of days, someone would be round, sniffing about and telling Dad he'd have to pay a fine. It was easy for the law to catch up with them too, now they were staying in one place.

Nicky stared at his hands, seeing the time stretch ahead – stuck at this school with the same jeers and jibes, day after day after day. He had never been at the same school for longer than six months in one stretch before. He was supposed to go when they weren't travelling, but sometimes – even when they weren't on the road – Dad or Grandad would keep him at home if they needed help with anything.

At those other schools, Nicky hardly ever mixed with the gorgios. There were always plenty of Gypsy friends to stick around with at Beech Forest. And at the other places, if there weren't other Gypsies about, he'd always known they were moving on. If things got rough, he didn't have to live with it for long.

Nicky closed his eyes, trying to shut it all away. But the thoughts stayed trapped in his head, everything closing round him like a cage.

Mr Nash spoke again. "What is the thing you hate most about coming here?"

Nicky glanced at him, then shrugged. He began to pick at a loose thread on the sleeve of his shirt. It was hard to choose.

Was it the work? He couldn't do it, and it made him feel hot and stupid when Miss Bullock gave him a worksheet and then left him with it. The stuff she gave him and Billy Clarke was supposed to be easier than the work everyone else got, but it still never made much sense. Then, when he got it wrong, she'd start shouting and say he was daydreaming instead of listening. Nicky was good with woodwork, and things with his hands, but Miss Bullock never gave him projects like that.

He pulled his mind back to Mr Nash's question: what did he hate most? Was it the others – their whispered laughter when he didn't know an answer? Or, like last week, when he got no marks in the spelling test?

Or was it Edward Carter? Always following him about, sniffing the air as if there was a bad smell whenever he came near, and calling him "Gyppo" like it was a swear word.

Nicky snapped the thread suddenly, feeling the sharp sting as it cut into his skin. "It's all the same, I s'pose. I hate everything." A thought flashed into his mind. "Couldn't I stay home and do it? You could send me books and stuff, and a teacher could come and visit me. I knew some Gypsies who learnt like that once."

Mr Nash shook his head. "I'm sorry, Nicky, but I don't think that would work. It's my job to keep you in school, to help you settle and become part of the community. Letting you stay away might just make things worse. Everyone would still think of you as being – well, different."

"But I *am* different. What's wrong with that?"

Mr Nash clenched his fingers tighter together, the knuckles flooding purple and then white. "It would be lovely if all the community could live and work happily side by side..."

"They hate us though," Nicky broke in. "Most

people round here want us gone. They say we're lazy, and we steal stuff…"

"I know what gets said. People don't always understand about other ways of living. It makes them feel suspicious, and scared."

"But we don't steal. Not all of us. And we work as hard as anyone, if we get the chance."

Mr Nash spoke gently. "In time, Nicky, people might come to realize that. But they have to get to know you properly first. And trying to punch Edward Carter on the nose isn't going to help."

Nicky didn't answer. A small spot of blood had bubbled up from the cut, and he stared down at it.

Mr Nash unlocked his fingers suddenly, and pushed a box of tissues across the desk. He watched Nicky dab at the blood. "OK, Nicky. I think I've kept you here long enough. You'd better get yourself back to class, and try and stay out of trouble for the rest of the day. Oh, and Nicky…"

"What?"

"I want to hear that you've apologized to Miss Bullock. I don't think calling her an 'old cow' is the best way to stay in her good books, do you?"

"But she—"

"No 'buts', Nicky. I'll support you all I can, but I can't help you if you don't help yourself."

Nicky looked back at him for a moment, imagining what it was going to feel like to have to go up to Miss Bullock with his tail between his legs. But then, Mr Nash was right. Miss Bullock was always snapping at his ankles. If he didn't say sorry, she might start going for his throat. "OK."

Mr Nash stood up. He walked round to Nicky and put his hand on his shoulder. Nicky flinched awkwardly and scraped back his chair, anxious to be gone.

Mr Nash let his hand drop back to his side, and cleared his throat. "Off you go then."

As he reached the door, Nicky glanced round. Mr Nash was standing watching him, and he nodded, giving Nicky a half smile.

Nicky hesitated for a moment, then smiled back. He was surprised to see a real warmth and understanding suddenly light up the head's tired eyes.

6

Nicky went back to Eclipse that night.

It had been a long, grotty day, with everyone whispering and giggling about him. Except for Edward. Edward just kept staring at him. A long, cold stare that Nicky could feel even when his back was turned. It made Nicky mad, being watched like that, and being with Eclipse was the best way he knew for getting all the muck out of his head.

For a long time he just rode her gently, walking her round and round the field, letting his mind soften and relax with the smooth sway of her body.

It was a misty evening. The trees loomed up like sudden ghosts. Once a rabbit scuttered in front of them. Once Nicky caught the gleam of a fox's eyes watching from the bushes.

Not once did Eclipse falter, or startle. Nicky spoke to her constantly, using old Gypsy words, his tone a cross between a whisper and a song. She flicked her ears, listening, and let the soft pressure of Nicky's legs, and the slight touch of his hands on her neck, tell her where to go.

The voices reached them suddenly. They came from a distance, somewhere back near the yard, but they carried easily across the quiet night.

It was Edward's voice. Edward and his dad. And they were arguing.

Very quietly, skirting the darkest edges of the field, Nicky guided Eclipse nearer.

"But my leg hurts. I can't do it again. We practised long enough last night."

"You've got to. You'll never be ready otherwise. Liam, Matt and Bretta can only do so much. Eclipse needs to know *you* again, not some stable hand."

"So why can't we wait till next season? Why is this year so important?"

"You can't afford to bow out of any year. Not if you're going to get to Olympic standard, like I did. And I've spent a lot on that horse. A lot in money, and a lot in time. This year's going to be crucial. Now get your hat, and wait for me in the indoor school. I'm going off to catch her."

Nicky slipped down from Eclipse's back and melted into the bushes, but he didn't leave. The mist was like a magic cloak to him, keeping him invisible.

He heard Declan Carter as he squelched across the field, his torch flashing, the yellow beam spreading strangely in the fuzzy light.

Eclipse heard him too. He was calling, rattling a bucket. She whickered softly, but stayed near Nicky.

"Come on, girl! There's work to do. Edward's waiting for you."

Nicky moved backwards as the dark shape of Declan Carter appeared from the mist, put a halter over Eclipse's head, and led her away.

He should have gone home then, but he didn't want to. He was curious, and he wanted to see how well Edward handled his horse.

Slipping behind them, Nicky followed as Declan Carter led Eclipse towards the indoor school.

There was a gap in the outside fence of the school; several planks had split away, and it was easy for Nicky to crouch in the damp grass and watch.

Edward's dad lunged her first, keeping her circling round and round on a long white rein. He held a whip in his right hand, and every time he cracked it, Nicky winced.

"About time too." Declan Carter didn't look round as Edward appeared by the gate. "I've warmed her up for you. She's all yours."

Nicky watched as Edward walked over to Eclipse, still on his crutches.

Nicky had always thought of Edward as tall, taller than anyone in their class, but tonight, standing helplessly beside Eclipse, with his dad coming across to push him up into the saddle, he suddenly looked very small.

"It hurts, Dad. It hurts to keep using my leg like this."

"You can't use your leg as an excuse for ever," Declan Carter growled. "You don't get to the top by whinging and whimpering. Just get on the horse. You'll soon get used to it." Declan Carter walked back the length of the leading rein and flicked the whip just behind Eclipse's hind legs. Her ears were back now, and she kept her head lowered, shaking it uncomfortably from side to side.

"Now trot."

"I can't, Dad. I don't want to."

"Don't waste time, Edward. I'm going away later tonight. We've got less than an hour to get this done."

In the floodlit school Nicky had a clear view of Edward's face. It was pinched and tight, and white with fear. He looked a different person from the one Nicky had almost punched at school earlier that day.

Declan Carter flicked the whip again, this time catching the back of Eclipse's hooves. She jumped in protest, nearly unseating Edward. Her tail had begun to swish, and her eyes were rolling backwards. Nicky could see the whites as she trotted past, her hooves pounding sharply in the white sand. She was beginning to sweat.

"Canter!"

"I can't. Let me get off. Leave me alone."

Nicky turned away, sickened, as Declan Carter cracked the whip again.

He could still hear the drum of hooves, and Edward whimpering, as he slipped back across the field to collect his bike.

He cycled furiously home down the misty lane, narrowly missing getting knocked down by a white car that screamed past suddenly, and trying to get the vision of the whip cutting across Eclipse's hooves out of his head.

Nicky locked his bike on to the tow-bar of Jim's trailer.

"You're late in. Where've you been?" Dad appeared in the doorway of his own trailer.

"Just out and about. Riding around."

"I hope it's just that bike you've been riding."

Nicky clicked shut the padlock, and didn't answer.

"And you shouldn't be going off on your own without telling anyone. Not round here."

Nicky straightened up, and looked across at Dad. It used to be Mum who was always fussing, wanting to know where he'd been, but Dad was the uptight one these days. "I can handle myself. You know I can."

Dad stared back at him for a moment, and when he finally spoke his voice seemed gruff and strange. "Get to bed now. You've got school in the morning." His trailer door banged shut behind him.

Nicky watched the closed door for a moment, before turning away. He gave a final check on his bike, ruffled Sky's ears, then climbed up into Jim's trailer.

Once inside, he folded down the seats to make his bed, and got his quilt from out of the cupboard.

He lay for a long time, watching the hazy half moon through the window, listening to Jim's ragged snores from the other side of the trailer, and running his mind back through everything he'd just seen at Edward's place.

7

"Remember, we're off to the pub soon." Mum looked up from dusting the china. "It's our night to eat out."

They'd started going to the "Pig and Whistle" every Friday since they'd settled here.

"Why do we have to keep going there?" Nicky flicked through the channels on the telly.

"You know it's a good way to mix and meet other gorgios," Dad grunted. "There's lots of them with farms and big gardens that go in there. The more we get in with them, the more chance we'll have of getting regular work."

"I'm staying here. I've got stuff to do for school." Nicky glanced at Mum. He knew she and Dad would give in to anything to do with school at the moment – they were too scared of getting called in and being told he wasn't coping. But he hated the hurt that shadowed Mum's eyes whenever he said he didn't want to go with them somewhere. They always used to go everywhere together.

The truth was, though, that Nicky hated being in the "Pig and Whistle" more than he hated upsetting Mum. As far as he could see, Dad's great plan of getting "in" with the locals was a flop. Although the couple that ran the pub were friendly, there were others in there who always stared at them, and sometimes even moved to another table if they thought the "Gyppos" were sitting too near.

Mum hesitated. "I don't like leaving you…"

"Jim's still around." Sabrina shot Nicky a look of support. "He's happier sitting outside with a can of beer and a fire going. Nicky can go over to him later."

"I just wish there were more people about to keep an eye on you. I never worried before…"

"Well, this isn't 'before', is it?"

Mum saw the warning spark of anger flash in Nicky's eyes, and gave in reluctantly. "No … I suppose not. But Jim's already eaten. I did him some sausages earlier, because I thought you'd be coming with us. Get yourself something if you're hungry. There's bacon in the fridge."

"And stay round here." Dad swung the pick-up

keys on one finger, his eyes narrowing. "If you let me down…"

"I'm not going anywhere." Nicky met the look squarely. "I told you, I'm doing my homework."

"If I get wind of any more trouble … if anyone else stops me and says their horse has been tied up and sprayed…"

"You – *you* can't think it was me!" Nicky felt like Dad had just rammed him in the gut.

"Just be where you're supposed to be, that's all I'm saying. That way, I won't have any explaining to do."

Dad turned and stomped outside to the pick-up. Mum shot Nicky a quick, anxious look, and then followed with Sabrina.

After a moment Nicky heard the engine start up, and they were gone.

He made himself a bacon sandwich and sat outside to eat it. The rain had stopped, and the evening smelt washed and warm. Feeling the restlessness begin to turn in him again, he threw the crusts to Sky, and walked across the squelching grass to the derelict garages at the edge of the site. He wouldn't go far, but he didn't fancy going over to Jim yet. The chances were he was probably asleep anyway.

In the trees that shaded the local tip the birds were returning for the night, twittering noisily as they gathered in the branches. It struck Nicky as odd that birds would sing so beautifully here.

Closing his eyes, he leant against a graffiti-scarred garage door and let the singing soak into him. Just for a moment, he could imagine the site at Beech Forest. When he was little, the birds there had always sounded like angels to him. He let his mind drift with the memory, seeing the trailers and the people, hearing the shouts and chatter of everyone coming together to talk about the day.

They'd been a bit like birds themselves in that way.

A white car swung suddenly into the back road and screeched to a halt beside him.

"All alone, Gyppo?" Edward Carter wound the window down and leaned out. Nicky recognized the driver as Liam Frazer, the stable hand from Edward's place. In the back sat his brother, Matt.

"What if I am?" Nicky scowled as Liam cut the engine, and he and Matt got out, walking over to Nicky and blocking him between the car and the garage door.

Edward stayed where he was.

"That wasn't a pretty scene in assembly yesterday morning," said Matt softly.

"And that wasn't a pretty attack on another horse last night either, over near Edward's place," added Liam.

57

"In fact, the whole thing was pretty ugly, considering it came from such a pretty boy." Edward was all mouth now. It was the old, bullying Edward again. There was no trace of the chalk-faced whimpering boy from the night before.

"I don't know anything about attacks on horses. I reckon that's more your dad's style." Nicky couldn't stop himself, remembering the whip cracking behind Eclipse's heels.

Edward's eyes became cold, hard slits. "What do you mean?"

Nicky could have kicked himself, realizing his mistake. "I've heard he trains hard, that's all."

"That's how he got to be an Olympic champion before he was twenty. Hard work and effort. Not like you, Gyppo. I doubt if you could win a donkey derby – unless you doped all the other donkeys first, of course." As Edward spoke, Nicky heard the echo of Declan Carter in his voice.

Liam cut in. "Anyway, what were you doing out on your own so late last night? I drove past you on my way back from town. You were cycling down that lane like the devil was chasing you."

Nicky shrugged. "I'd been out. Looking around."

"I bet you had, Gyppo. Looking for horses to terrify the hell out of." Edward smiled smugly as he spoke. Nicky longed to take that smugness out of

58

his thin, sneering face. He longed to spit out to Liam and Matt where he'd really been. What he'd really been watching. He had a feeling neither of them knew about Edward's special training sessions at night.

But he couldn't risk saying anything more. Not if he wanted to go to Eclipse again. And he wasn't going to gamble with anything that might make Edward suspicious. "Just leave me alone," he muttered.

"With pleasure, Gyppo." Edward spoke slowly. "But if we hear of one more horse being attacked, you'll have us to answer to." Edward nodded at Liam and Matt, and they got back in the car, reversing noisily, the tyres squealing as they sped away.

As he walked quickly back towards the trailers, Nicky told himself it was anger that was making him shake all over. Not fear.

8

The loud disco beat bugged Nicky as soon as he arrived. It was noisy and droning. Girls stood in huddled circles, dancing together and giggling. Boys hung round the edge of the hall, throwing crisps at each other or just trying to look cool.

It was the termly school disco, and Nicky hated it.

"I'll wait outside. Come and find me when it finishes." Nicky had to bend forward and shout in Sabrina's ear.

"You can't go," she shouted back. "I need you to stay and dance. No one else will ask me."

"Don't push it, Sabrina. I only came because Mum said you couldn't come without me. You know what I think about stuff like this."

"OK." Sabrina rolled her eyes upwards. "I'll just have to dance on my own."

Nicky didn't leave straight away. He leaned against the wall at the back of the hall, watching his sister. He had to give it to her – Sabrina might be behind at reading and maths, but she wasn't scared of letting herself go on the dance floor. Pushing through the clusters of jiggling girls, she began her own dance, right in the middle of the hall. It was a wild, exuberant twisting and spinning, as if all the music was alive and pulsing through her.

And it must have got through to the others, because a boy from further up the school went to join her, and gradually all the girls broke out of their circles and began to try different steps and movements of their own.

From across the hall Nicky felt someone watching him. Turning quickly, his eyes locked with Bretta's. She was standing on her own over by the drinks hatch, looking older than usual. Her hair was brushed, and she was wearing a strappy blue dress. Normally she only wore trousers, even for school.

Suddenly, to his embarrassment, she gave him a shy smile and came across.

She stood squarely in front of him and took a deep breath, as if she was about to make a speech. She had to lean close to make herself heard above the throb of music. "I wanted to say that I'm sorry."

"What about?" It was difficult trying to sound sullen, shouting back into her ear.

Bretta looked away, then back at Nicky. "I had no right to come round accusing you that time. I just got all wound up talking to Edward. He was sure it was you who'd sprayed that horse, and I wasn't thinking straight. Especially after catching you on Eclipse the night before. But Edward, he's sort of – well, he's got something against you, for some reason."

"That's one way of putting it." The music stopped while the DJ announced a dance competition, and they could talk normally for a moment.

"Well, anyway, I wish I hadn't said it now. I suppose I just get carried away when I hear about people hurting horses."

Nicky looked at her. She seemed flustered, and his eyes softened. "I know. I get like that too."

They stood awkwardly, watching the dancing as the music began again.

Then Bretta leaned back across to Nicky. "You OK?"

"Why shouldn't I be?"

"Well, I guess this isn't really your idea of a wild night out."

"Is it yours then?"

She smiled again, a bigger smile this time. It lit

up her whole face. "Not much. But I promised Edward I'd come. He doesn't manage very well on his own."

Nicky was about to answer when something – a feeling – made him glance round. Over near the hall door stood Edward Carter, watching them intently. He didn't look pleased.

Bretta saw him too. "I've got to go." She squeezed Nicky lightly on the arm, and hurried over to Edward. They walked together towards the chairs that lined the far side of the hall, and sat down.

Suddenly the music, and the people, and the smell of sweat, were all too much for Nicky.

He turned away and slipped outside into the school grounds.

It was a clear, beautiful night. Thousands of stars winked and glittered in the inky sky. A gibbous moon hung silver over the school playing fields, wisps of cloud throwing shadows across it as they passed.

Nicky sat on a bench at the edge of the path, trying to ignore the relentless disco beat that rolled towards him out of the open windows. He wondered why it was that Bretta Miles should waste her time on a jerk like Edward. Unless it was because staying in with Edward was a way of making certain she could keep riding Eclipse. Still, even that didn't quite fit. Bretta didn't seem like the sort of person who'd creep round someone she didn't like, just to get something she wanted.

Nicky picked up a fallen twig from the ground and began peeling tiny pieces of bark off with his fingernail.

He snapped the twig fiercely, then threw the pieces hard in the direction of the building.

He felt suddenly restless. There was energy buzzing through him. He got up and began pacing round the edge of the field like a caged animal. The restless feeling grew. He wanted something. He wanted action. He wanted excitement. And more than anything else, he wanted the fast, heart-hammering thrill of riding Eclipse.

He glanced up at the moon. Eclipse's field was a good hour's walk away from the school. He wouldn't have time to get there and back *and* have a decent ride before the disco ended.

But he had to go somewhere, and it had to be with horses, even it was just for a little while.

Suddenly he remembered Badger Farm Riding Stables. That was only thirty minutes away, provided he ran. He'd hung round there a lot when they first moved here, before he discovered Eclipse.

He always went at night, when the stables were shut, and the ponies had been let out into the fields. It was great, the animals nuzzling round him, all of them anxious to be patted and stroked. Sometimes he rode them, but only when it felt right. To his mind riding-school ponies worked hard enough all day, and earned whatever rest they could get.

Nicky arrived at the stables sweating, but calmer. Just the idea of being near horses had settled him. Ducking through a gap in the hedge, he stood in the field and whistled softly. The ponies were gathered together under the trees at the top end, and as he watched Nicky could see them pressing together. Even from a distance he could sense they were restless. When he whistled they looked towards him, but they didn't come over. Nicky thought it was odd. They usually came straight away.

Keeping to the shadows, Nicky slipped round, getting slowly nearer to the ponies. They kept watching him, their eyes glowing strangely in the dark. As he got level with them he crossed over, till he was standing amongst them. He touched each forehead gently, whispering. Their ears flicked towards him, and they snorted soft greetings, but they still seemed edgy and unsure.

Out in the lane a car door slammed. Nicky stiffened. It would be just his luck if the stable owner came to do a night-time check. But then an engine started up, and Nicky relaxed again. Whoever it was must be going, not coming.

There was a black pony nuzzling him, pushing its nose into his back. Nicky laughed quietly and rubbed its mane. Its dark colouring reminded him of Eclipse. He wrapped his arms around the pony's neck, and it leaned against him. Slowly Nicky felt all the tension lift out of it, like a cloud passing away. And as the black pony relaxed, Nicky felt all the others settle too, as if some secret message had passed between them.

"Come on," Nicky whispered suddenly, "just for five minutes. It'll do us both good." And he swung up on to its back.

The pony moved easily round and round the field, first walking, then trotting, then finally, at Nicky's gentle urging, breaking into a thundering gallop. Behind them, Nicky could hear the *thud*, *thud*, *thud* of other hooves. The others were following. Glancing back Nicky felt a wild exhilaration. It was brilliant – him racing along in front, and twenty or more other ponies chasing behind!

Then, all of a sudden, the black pony stopped dead. The others stopped too, pressing and knocking against Nicky's legs, almost making him fall. He slid down from the pony's back and stood quietly. They were all restless again, even worse than before. And whatever it was, Nicky could sense it too. The strong smell of fear, not from the ponies now, but from something else, seemed to hang in the air.

Nicky walked forward slowly, and the feeling grew. He felt strange. Almost sick. There was something very wrong.

Then he saw it: a stone-grey pony standing rigid, like a statue, amongst a small copse of trees. But it wasn't just the still, frozen way it was standing that jolted Nicky. It was the menace that hung round it, as if the energy that had caused this was alive and buzzing. Nicky broke into a run. The pony started suddenly, as if a spell had been broken. It half-reared, and tried to jump sideways, away from him. But as it moved it stumbled and almost fell. Its head jabbed the air with a frightened jerk. It neighed sharply, a half-scream, and Nicky saw the white glint on its face as it rolled its eyes in panic.

"Steady. Steady." His hands touched its sides, bending down to see what had caught it. "Oh Christ," he muttered. "Not you as well!" The pony's back legs were bound tightly with stringy rope. Then, as he ran his fingers across its trembling body, he felt the damp, sticky touch of paint. He traced it with his fingers. It was the same shape. Like the "Z" that Bretta had shown him in the newspaper. Only this time it had been done differently – the lines vertical instead of horizontal. This time, it was quite clearly the letter "N".

"Stand easy," he murmured gently. "I'll sort you out. This must really be cutting into you." Nicky knelt and struggled to untie the knots. The pony became still again. It was blowing hard, its breath coming like a frightened wheeze in its throat, but it seemed to understand that he was trying to help. "I can't do anything about the paint," Nicky said at last, winding the rope round his wrist as he straightened up, "but I'll think of a way to get help out here. Maybe I'll even phone the gavvers."

Nicky had never in his life contacted the police before, but this was important. The animal was still terrified, and if it tried to chew at the paint on its side, it could poison itself. Nicky knew horses were always in danger from anything toxic because they couldn't vomit, like most other animals could. They had a muscle in front of their stomach which stopped the food from coming back up.

But it didn't matter because suddenly, from across the field, he heard voices and saw lights flashing.

There wasn't any need for him to go contacting the police. The police were coming to him.

And as the first one reached him and ran his torchlight over the frightened pony, the paint mark on its side, and the rope round Nicky's wrist, Nicky knew that things didn't look too good.

9

"**M**ove away from the horse!"

"It wasn't me. I was just—"

"Save it, kid." One of the officers took the rope from Nicky's hands.

The other went over to the pony, reaching his arm towards it and clucking with his tongue. "Here, horse. Steady, horse."

The pony started sideways, half-rearing. The policeman jumped back. "Poor thing. It's frightened to death. Won't let me near it."

"Just stay with it then. We've contacted the owner. They'll be here in a minute."

The first policeman took hold of Nicky's arm. "I'm arresting you on suspicion of criminal damage. We'll be taking you down to the station, and we'll get a full statement from you there. I suggest you come quietly. It'll make all of our lives a lot easier."

The policeman led Nicky across the shadowed field, the torchlight beaming a dancing white path ahead of them. He kept a tight grip on Nicky's arm, but he needn't have. Nicky knew there wasn't any point in running.

Back at the yard, the lights were on everywhere. A horse was kicking at the door of its stable, unsettled by the commotion. Two Red Setters raced down the yard, barking wildly at Nicky and the policeman.

A woman hurried out from a door marked "Office". "So you've got him then." She stared at Nicky in the artificial light, her eyes narrow and hard.

The policeman kept his hold on Nicky, and held out his other hand towards the woman. "I'm Inspector Whymark. My colleague, Sergeant Simms, is with the horse. It seems a bit upset. We thought it was best to let you deal with it."

"My daughter's already gone. She drove round in the Land Rover. It's quicker that way."

The woman stepped closer, so close that Nicky could see the deep lines of weather and age that criss-crossed her face. So close that he could smell the cigarette smoke on her breath. "You disgust me." She had a harsh, deep voice, almost like a man.

"How could you do that to an innocent, trusting animal?"

"I—"

"Don't speak! I don't want to hear anything you've got to say."

She clenched her fist and Nicky flinched, ducking his head slightly, afraid she might hit him.

As his eyes jerked sideways, he realized there was somebody else in the yard.

Somebody standing watching.

It was Bretta Miles.

"What are you doing here?" Surprise made the question burst out of him.

Bretta walked nearer. She looked pale and tense. "I followed you." Her voice was like ice.

"But you were at the disco with Edward."

"Not for long. Edward's leg was bothering him. It kept getting knocked, so we went and sat outside for a while. He saw you creeping about in the school playing field."

Nicky stood sullenly, hating the idea of being watched without knowing it.

Inspector Whymark, one hand still gripping Nicky's arm, had turned away slightly and was answering a crackled message on his walkie-talkie.

Bretta went on. "He said he was sure you were up to something. He even said he thought you might be coming here, because it was the nearest place with horses. He reckoned you'd do anything to get at horses. He says it's a problem with you. Like a madness."

Sudden anger cut through Nicky, and for a moment he forgot where he was, and why. "I'm deeply touched that he's taken the trouble to get to know me so well."

Bretta's voice quivered. "It's a good job he did, isn't it?"

Nicky's eyes locked with hers. He felt a fresh rage lurch through him, that she should be so quick to run to Edward's side again. "So where's wonder boy now? Why isn't he with you, helping to save Maybridge from hordes of villainous gypsies?"

"He got ill after that. He's on tablets to take the pain away from his leg, and they make him go a bit funny sometimes."

"You're telling me," Nicky muttered.

Bretta ignored him. "He had his mobile with him. His dad's gone away till next week, so he rang Liam to come and take him home again. Liam's a sort of taxi service for Edward when his dad's not there."

"A private chauffeur. Lucky old Edward. And I s'pose Uncle Liam's babysitting for him too?"

"No. Liam was going straight out afterwards. Edward will be on his own. I'm going over to see him in a minute. Oh, I don't know what I'm telling you this for. I don't even know why I'm talking to you..." She turned away sharply, her shoulders hunched tightly as if she was locking up her whole body against him.

Nicky tried to shrug. He wasn't going to bother to explain what had really happened. It would just give her more to feed Edward with when she went to see him. But inside he felt a dull, unexpected ache. As if he had just lost something that might have been precious.

At that moment Sergeant Simms came back. He nodded at the owner. "Horse seems a bit calmer. It jumped about a bit at first, but your daughter's with it. She said she'll walk it back here as soon as it seems quiet enough."

Inspector Whymark pulled at Nicky's arm. "OK, horse nut. Let's get you back to the station. You can tell us all about it from there."

As Nicky walked between the two officers towards the police car, Bretta ran up behind them suddenly. "I wanted Edward to be wrong about you. I wanted to be able to get him to leave you alone. That was why I followed you." As Nicky stopped to stare at her, Bretta's face suddenly crumpled and she burst into tears.

Nicky climbed into the back of the car, feeling as sick as if he'd just had a gutful of sour milk forced down his throat.

10

"Empty your pockets, please."

Nicky fumbled and found a half-pack of chewing gum, and handed it to the sandy-haired police officer at the station.

"Name and address?"

Nicky mumbled his answers as the policeman fired questions, gave him forms to fill in that he couldn't read, and rattled on about "rights" and "evidence".

Nicky hardly listened. His hands shook when he scrawled his name along the bottom of the forms, and his eyes kept catching the heavy metal handcuffs hanging from the policeman's belt.

He was led down a long, thin corridor to a cell.

They stopped by a heavy grey door.

"Please remove your laces."

Nicky frowned, but bent to unthread the laces in his trainers. He noticed, as he did so, other laces left outside other grey doors, all in untidy huddles down the corridor.

The policeman took a giant silver key, and unlocked the door. He pushed it open and led Nicky inside. "Ring the buzzer if you need anything." He pointed to a red button on the wall. "We'll be contacting your parents. Then we'll sort you out properly."

The door slammed with a hollow clang, and Nicky was on his own.

There was just a hard wooden bench with a plastic mattress, and a toilet. There was no door to shut off the toilet. The whole room smelt funny, and Nicky realized it was a revolting mix of disinfectant and urine. The thick glass bricks of the window gave Nicky no hint of the world outside.

Sounds were muffled, but from time to time Nicky heard footsteps and shouts, and once the harsh retching of someone throwing up.

He sat hunched on the bench, his arms hugged tight to his chest, trying not to think. But the panic was rising. He felt sticky-hot and shaky. His skin prickled, as if insects were running across him, and he couldn't breathe. All around him, the walls were closing in.

Nicky squeezed his eyes shut, but that was worse. The room seemed to lurch, and he thought he might be sick. He pushed his hands hard against his head, telling himself it would stop soon. Telling himself it was all in his mind. Lifts, trains, anything he couldn't get out of, always pressed into him like this.

The only time he could ever remember crying in front of anyone else was when a group of girls at one of his old schools trapped him in a cupboard. They stayed outside, sitting in chairs wedged up hard against the door. Nicky could still remember the sound of their laughter, like something in a bad dream. In the end they let him out, but only because his screams were so loud they got scared a teacher might hear.

Nicky didn't cry this time, but he was shaking hard and sickly white when Mum finally arrived and he was led out to the interview room.

"This interview is being tape-recorded. I am Police Constable Bevis, and I am interviewing Nicky Ghiselli. Please give your full name and date of birth."

Nicky answered dully, still dazed from the cell. The policeman spoke in a clipped, cold voice, reciting the time, the place, and something about legal advice.

Mum sat opposite Nicky, twisting her hands anxiously. She looked as bad as Nicky felt. Still, he was glad it was Mum who'd come. It was Friday night, and Mum and Dad had been at the "Pig and Whistle". The police must have gone into the pub to tell them. Nicky couldn't imagine Dad taking it too well.

"Now then, Nicky, could you explain, in your own words, exactly what you were doing in that field?"

"I was going for a walk." Nicky kept his head down and mumbled into his lap.

"At night?"

"I often do it. I like the dark."

"Your mother told us it couldn't have been you we'd picked up, because you were with your sister at the school disco. She thought someone must be setting you up." PC Bevis glanced at his notes. "Maybridge School is a good thirty minutes from Badger Farm Riding Stables. So what happened? Were you practising fox-trotting in the fields, or something?"

"I told you, I was just going for a walk. I don't like discos."

"So how was it you ended up at Badger Farm?"

"I like horses. I like being near them." Nicky met PC Bevis's steady gaze. "Is that a crime?"

"Not on its own." PC Bevis leant across the table

towards him. "But perhaps you could explain about the rope you were holding at the time we found you?"

"I'd just untied it from the horse's legs."

"The animal was standing in a very shadowy corner of that field. It seems odd that you knew it was there."

Nicky hesitated, remembering the wild ride across the fields, the ponies galloping behind, their sudden frightened halt as they neared the trees. How could he explain how he'd found that stone-grey pony, without telling the rest?

He shrugged. "I dunno. I just suddenly saw it."

"So you were just walking happily through a dark field, when all of a sudden you saw a horse, and you thought 'good heavens, I wonder if that animal has been tied up by someone,' so you went over to check and – surprise surprise – it had been. How lucky that you just happened to be there to help it."

"I knew it was there. The horse sort of – called me."

"You mean it's a talking horse?"

"No – I mean – I just feel things from horses."

"It's true." Mum spoke for the first time. "He's got a gift with horses."

"I must ask you not to interrupt." PC Bevis was speaking to Mum, but his eyes were still fixed on Nicky, and when he spoke again his voice had a new edge to it. "So you've got a gift. You talk to horses, and horses come to you. Is that what you're saying?"

Nicky nodded, looking up at him for the first time. "Sort of." Perhaps PC Bevis would understand. Perhaps it might be worth telling the truth.

"So that must make it very easy."

"Make what very easy?"

"To get close. Close enough to tie them up. Close enough to spray paint on them."

It was as if PC Bevis had slapped him. "I didn't do it. Horses trust me. Take me back there now, and I'll show you how they are with me. Horses can smell danger. Horses know what evil is. If you watched them with me, you'd know…"

PC Bevis sighed. "You've got to admit it, Nicky, it all seems pretty odd from where I'm sitting. You even left your signature on the horse."

"It's not my signature. It looks like an 'N', but it could be a 'Z', or a snake, or anything."

"So even in the dark you knew exactly what shape that horse had got sprayed across its rump."

Nicky felt the hole he was digging himself into get deeper and deeper. "I read about it. It was in the paper."

"Funny, that. You told us you couldn't read much when we first brought you in, when we needed you to sign our forms."

Nicky ran his hands through his hair and stared down at the brown cord carpet on the floor. There wasn't any point going on with this. There wasn't anything he could say.

There was a long pause, then PC Bevis asked quietly, "Do you wish to clarify anything you have said?"

"No."

"Do you wish to add anything?"

"Only that it wasn't me. I didn't do it." Nicky's voice was muffled and small.

PC Bevis sighed, and switched back into the clipped, official tone he had used at the beginning. "The time is 22.07 hours, and I am switching the recorder off."

He turned back to Nicky. "You were lucky this time. We haven't found any proper evidence – it's all just circumstantial. And unlike you, we can't talk to horses, so we can't check your story with them. But remember – we treat horses like property in an incident like this, and a charge of criminal damage carries a penalty of up to ten years."

Nicky noticed the carpet was worn, the cord rubbed away in places. He pictured all the other feet – shoplifters' feet, burglars' feet, murderers' feet – that might have been where his were now.

PC Bevis leaned closer. "We'll be watching you. We know a bit about you. And if anything else odd happens – especially with horses – we might just be popping round to see what you were doing at the time."

"You mean he's free to go?" Mum spoke suddenly, unable to keep the surprised note from her voice.

"For now, yes. I just need him to sign this form, we'll go back out to the desk, and he'll be released with no further action. The horse's owner may want to bring a private prosecution for trespass, but we've finished with him."

PC Bevis leaned back in his chair. "But don't let him prowl about at night on his own any more. Any more strange incidents and we'll be down on him like a mountain of manure."

Ten minutes later Nicky was re-united with his laces and chewing gum, and he and Mum were headed home.

They walked apart from each other, and they didn't speak.

11

Dad, on the other hand, had plenty to say.
He said it with the back of his hand first,
something he hadn't done since he'd found Nicky
taking sweets from a jar in one of Grandad's
cupboards when he was about six.

Nicky went reeling across the trailer, shocked and
sickened.

Mum and Sabrina had been sent to sit with Jim.

"So what the hell did you think you were
doing?"

"I was riding, that's all. I just found the horse tied
up, I undid the rope, and the gavvers came along. I
was unlucky."

"Unlucky? Is that what you call it. You were
damn stupid!"

"But it's the horses." Nicky stuck his chin out defiantly. "You know I can't be without them."

"You'll be without any skin on your backside if I catch you sneaking anywhere near horses again! You're staying in from now on, every night – where your mum and I can keep an eye on you. We can do without you bringing trouble on us. I'll drive you to school, and I'll pick you up, and you can stay in the trailer every evening unless I need you for something."

Nicky stared at him. They'd always backed each other up against outsiders. It was Gypsy code. Even after the big fight with Grandad, Nicky would never have dreamed of griping about Dad to anyone outside the family, even though it had caused them so much grief. And in the old days Dad would have said that the police were wrong. Or that Bretta did it. Or that Nicky was set up. Even if it *was* Nicky's fault. Now it seemed he was happy to chuck him to the lions, just the same as everyone else.

"Now get next door to bed. I'm going out, and you'd better still be in there when I get back."

Nicky heard the door of the trailer slam, and then the roar and screech of the pick-up as it pulled away.

Mum and Sabrina were sitting with Jim round the fire outside, talking in quiet whispers, as if they were sharing secrets. Only Sky, curled up between them, looked round and thumped her tail as Nicky walked past.

He climbed into Jim's trailer, pulled his quilt from the cupboard, opened the seat out, and went to bed.

Some time later Jim came in and started clattering about by the sink, making himself a drink. He still didn't speak to Nicky.

Pulling his quilt up tight round him, Nicky lay facing the wall.

After a while, he heard Jim pull his own bed out and climb in. His snores rasped through the quiet within five minutes.

Later, much later, Nicky heard the pick-up come back, and Mum and Dad's raised voices from the trailer next door.

So even they were fighting now. They hardly ever did that.

Nicky turned over, staring up at the ceiling. Everything was wrong. Their lives were full of shadows. Nothing was like it used to be, and it never would be again.

The shouting stopped, and everything went quiet.

And in the silence, Nicky allowed himself to feel how much he hated it in Maybridge. The place. The school. The people.

He could only breathe if he could be near horses.

If Dad kept him trapped in here, he might as well have gone to prison.

He sat up suddenly. He wouldn't do it. He wouldn't live like that.

There was only one thing he could do.

12

Nicky didn't take much.

He couldn't risk rummaging about for too long. Jim usually slept like the dead, but it would be just Nicky's luck if he had a sudden attack of insomnia.

Moving quietly, he emptied his school rucksack out on to the bed, shoved a few clothes inside, and added crisps and coke from the kitchen cupboard. Jim didn't keep much food – he relied on what Mum did for him from the other trailer – but Nicky always made sure they had a few bits and pieces, in case he got hungry in the night.

Then he took fifty pounds in cash from the tin Jim always kept in an empty cereal packet. There was more in there – loads more – but fifty was plenty for what he wanted.

Sky thumped her tail and pressed her wet nose against his face as he bent to hug her goodbye. Nicky could hear her whimpering softly, straining on her rope as she watched him slip away into the darkness.

It was thirty minutes' fast walking from the trailers to Eclipse's field, and the opposite direction from the way Nicky needed to go, but he didn't care. He needed to see her one last time before he left for good.

It was a warm night, muggy, with the threat of storm in the air. Nicky got hot, and his shirt was sticking to him by the time he reached the field.

He waited in the shadows, giving the soft call in his throat that always got Eclipse trotting over. She didn't come.

Anxious, he flitted quietly around the edge of the field, checking amongst the trees and the furthest corners. Nothing stirred. The smell of the storm was stronger now, and even the foxes were lying low.

Then he remembered Edward's words: *We'll have to keep her stabled while there's a mystery madman about.*

So that would be it. She'd be somewhere over in the yard.

It was risky, but he had to find her to say goodbye.

Moving like a shadow, he slunk across the fields towards the buildings.

There was a security light hung above the door of the tack room. Nicky kept low, and it didn't come on. The only other light was the distant glow from the porch outside Edward's front door. Liam's place – the converted railway carriage – was in darkness.

Inside their stables the horses were restless. He could hear them snort and whicker, calling to him and to each other as he went by. In the wild, horses huddle close as a storm approaches, and Nicky knew that they were all nervous and uneasy being separated from each other.

He wished he could go in to each of them, rub their foreheads and settle them down, but there wasn't time. He crept on, pausing at each door, listening carefully.

At last he heard her. Nicky knew her call like some mothers know the cry of their own baby from a hundred others.

Very carefully he slid back the bolt on the lower door, pulling it shut behind him as he slipped through.

Outside, the first rumble of thunder shook the night.

The dark was so thick Nicky could almost feel it. There was nothing to see but blackness. But Eclipse knew it was him. She knew from his smell, and from the way he moved, in the same way that Nicky knew her.

She pressed her head into his shoulder, blowing against him, making soft smacking noises with her lips. Nicky blew softly too, then ran his hands all across her, his fingers scratching and digging into the warm velvet of her coat. His movements were a grooming action, the way horses groom each other, and Eclipse responded by twisting her neck round, trying to nibble and pick at his clothes with her teeth. She was grooming him back.

Outside a hard rain had begun to rattle the stable roof. The thunder smacked into the sky again, and through the gap that ran under the door, Nicky saw white flashes of lightning.

On either side of them horses were kicking and calling. Nicky and Eclipse stood silent, leaning into each other, safe and calm together.

Suddenly, in the quiet between the thunder, Nicky heard another sound.

It was the deep, rattling growl of a car engine. Someone was driving up to the stables from the lower end, the end where he and Dad had cleared the brick rubble away. For a moment the car stopped, its engine ticking over, then came the unmistakable whine of the automatic garage door being opened.

Declan Carter! It had to be. He was obviously getting home late.

Nicky's heart hammered. He only had a moment,

and Declan Carter would be walking back up the stable yard – maybe doing a late night check on his horses – maybe noticing that Eclipse's stable door wasn't properly shut...

Giving Eclipse one last, fierce hug, Nicky slipped away, sliding the bolt across quietly to shut the door, and melting into the bushes in the field opposite.

He was only just in time. As he crouched low amongst the leaves, the rain seeping in through his sweatshirt and jeans, he heard the garage door whine closed again.

Then there were footsteps, squelching along the puddled yard back up towards the house. Nicky kept very still, not even lifting his head to watch as Declan Carter hurried by.

It wasn't until the footsteps faded, and Nicky was certain that Edward's dad was a safe distance away, that he let himself straighten up.

The rain was everywhere. Down his back, in his eyes, on his nose. Nicky wiped his hand across his face and glanced towards the disappearing figure.

His hand stopped, frozen in mid-air.

A sheet of lightning lit up the whole yard, the centre of it slicing through the sky behind the bungalow. And in the sudden light, Nicky saw clearly the figure that was heading away from him. There was no mistaking it. It wasn't Declan Carter. It was Edward.

13

Nicky couldn't hang about. For some reason Declan Carter must still be down in the garage, but he might come out at any minute. He might even check the fields. If he'd been nervous enough to keep the horses shut in, he could decide to have a good look around before he went back indoors.

Nicky crept away, listening all the time for the opening whine of the garage door. It didn't come, and he was soon out of earshot, slipping back across Eclipse's field and over the five-barred gate into the lane.

He walked fast, trying to put everything behind him, but the image of Edward nagged for a long time. There was something odd about him just now. Something different. But however many times

Nicky ran the scene through, he couldn't work out what it was.

In the end he gave up. He was getting out, away from all of it. It was a waste of time puzzling over Edward. He was just a jerk, and if Nicky had his way he'd never see him again.

Except that the relief Nicky felt about not seeing Edward was suddenly shadowed by the thought that, if he never saw Edward, he would never see Eclipse again either. And thinking about that was like a hammer knocking nails into his chest.

It was a long night. The rain slowed and eventually stopped, but everything about him was drenched. His clothes clung to him, and the damp soaked through to his skin. In spite of the warm air, Nicky shivered as he walked.

At last, tired and aching, he turned down a gravel track. It was marked "private" – a sign he knew well from travelling days – but that was what Nicky wanted. He needed to be somewhere where other people weren't likely to come.

Melting into the darkness of a small wood he stopped at last, flopped down on the soft moss between the feet of a giant oak, and slept.

When he woke it was morning, and very warm.

He moved from the shade of the wood out towards the light.

Ahead was a small lake. The banks that ran down to it were steep, but round the edge he could see pockets of grass that shone bright in the sun.

It was what he needed: somewhere hidden, where he could sort himself out. A boy in wet clothes might attract odd questions and stares. He needed time to dry everything before he set off again.

Nicky half ran, half slid down the muddy slope. Then, peeling off his clinging wet things and draping everything on branches, he settled in a patch of warmth and watched the ducks that dipped and dived across the quiet water.

The shadows moved round, and a soft afternoon breeze blew ripples of silver across the lake.

Nicky sat up and sorted out his clothes. Everything was dry, so he dressed, packed his rucksack, and feasted on coke and crisps. The ducks swam towards him, honking and jostling, their bright eyes watching hopefully.

Nicky laughed. "You're out of luck, mates. Crisps will give you tummy ache, and I haven't got anything else."

A raggy brown duck with half a wing missing didn't seem to believe him. She floated to the edge of the lake and waddled nearer. The others pushed closer. The brown duck nudged Nicky all over, climbing across his legs as if they were logs. Nicky sat very still, letting her explore him, careful not to frighten her. A couple of others began climbing out of the water to join her.

Nicky was so caught up watching the ducks that he didn't hear the footsteps. Not until it was too late.

"Hey, you!"

Nicky jumped, a shower of crisps scattering from the bag. The ducks, fluttering and flustered, scrabbled back into the water and swam away.

"Can't you read? This is private property." A man was leaning over him from the top of the bank. He was old – as old as Grandad – but his face was scrunched up and bitter. He looked as if he'd spent all of his life being cross. Beside him a silky black spaniel barked twice, then whined softly, licking her lips and staring out over the lake.

Nicky hesitated, wondering how he was going to get past. He could only go up. The bushes close by were too thick, and there was only the water behind him. "I – I got lost."

The man scowled. "People who get lost don't usually slide down muddy banks to have a picnic. You're trespassing here. I've got a good mind to call the police."

The mention of the police sent a jolt of panic through Nicky. He remembered PC Bevis's last words. *Any more strange incidents, and we'll be down on him like a mountain of manure...*

"I'll go. My mum's expecting me. I – I'm sorry."
Nicky hated the last bit. He hated saying sorry to a
gorgio. It was OK if he'd done something wrong,
but he was just sitting there, drying out. And he
hated this crabby old man owning all this beautiful
place, then stopping anyone else from enjoying it.

He hoisted his rucksack over his back and
scrambled up the slope. The man was still scowling.
Nicky noticed he'd taken a mobile phone from his
pocket.

"I said I'm going, OK."

As he reached the top of the bank, the man
stepped into his path, grabbing his shoulder. "I
don't think so," he growled. "I've had enough of
you kids. Creeping about in here, frightening the
birds, leaving your rubbish everywhere…"

Nicky flushed. There were two empty coke cans
left at the bottom of the bank. "You startled me.
Normally I clean up."

The man kept moaning on, as if he didn't even
hear him. "You kids today just don't care. Those
cans could damage birds, or fish. You've got no
respect for anything."

Nicky faced him, about to say sorry again, when
he noticed a long, slim canvas bag slung over the
man's shoulder. A gun.

Suddenly he was furious. This miserable old
piker who was going on at him about coke cans was

probably going to spend the rest of the afternoon making ducks fall out of the sky. He wrenched his arm away suddenly. "Get off me! And don't worry, I wouldn't want to come near you again in a million years." Nicky raised his fist for a second and the man stepped back, his face darkening. Nicky took his chance, and ran.

As he pushed his way back through the wood, down the gravel path and out onto the road, he heard the echoing blast of gunshot and the frightened call of the ducks – again, and again, and again.

Nicky hoped the raggy brown duck could swim faster than she could fly.

14

Back out on the road, he kept heading west towards the next town.

He knew the way. It was a route they'd travelled often, at least once a year. It was the road that led to the horse fair, and the old life he was going back to.

The late afternoon sky was soft denim blue. Buds hung like green jewels from the branches of trees. Wild daffodils splashed yellow amongst the grass verges, and from the fields came the gentle bleating of sheep and lambs. Nicky suddenly felt good. Once he met up with Grandad, everything would fall into place. He'd be back with horses. He'd be back with his own people. He'd be back where he belonged.

Swinging his arms, he walked faster.

"Chicken and chips, and a giant Pepsi."

Nicky paid for the food and ate it hungrily, walking along the cobbled streets of a small market town. Then he found a supermarket and stocked up with as much bread and cold meat, chocolate and drink, as he could cram into the rucksack.

It was dusk when he left the town and set off into open countryside again.

The going was tougher than he'd expected. The twists and turns of the road slowed him down. The endless hills pulled at the muscles in the back of his legs. It would take for ever at this rate, and he didn't have for ever to spare. The fair started on Wednesday – just five days away. He couldn't risk arriving too late. It was his one chance to meet up with the others – after they left the fair, there would be no telling where they'd head for this time of year.

The road was busy. He had to stop for cars racing past him all the time, forcing him up on to banks and verges.

Suddenly he heard the rattle of a pick-up winding up the hill towards him. His heart stopped. Dad! In panic, he squeezed between a clump of brambles and a barbed wire fence. Through a gap in the branches he watched the pick-up shoot by. It was blue, and very rusty. It wasn't Dad at all.

Nicky unhooked a spike of broken wire from his torn sleeve. His hands and face were scratched and stinging. But what was worse was that, next time, there might not be any brambles to hide in. And next time it might really be Dad.

He wondered about Dad, Mum, and Sabrina. Up until now, he'd pushed them from his mind. Dad was probably still mad at him. Mum would be upset. Both of them would know he could cope on his own, so they probably weren't losing sleep about that, but either way his disappearing wasn't likely to make him a hot favourite. And Nicky couldn't face being picked up by Dad before he'd sorted things out. He had to get to Grandad first. After that, he'd face the rest of them.

He decided cross–country would be safer – walking across the fields and hills. But even then it was a hard slog. His feet were aching, he had blisters and sores, and he felt dirty and tired.

He stopped by a derelict barn, half tempted to spend the night there. Perhaps he should give up the whole idea, and slink back home with his tail between his legs after all.

Suddenly he heard a sound: the familiar tread of hooves coming towards him. He'd been so washed out, he hadn't even realized there was a pony here.

It was a chestnut, just a youngster, with a splash of white marking his face, and four white stockings that spread up almost to his belly.

"Hey there!" Nicky got up to greet him, feeling

as if he'd come across an old friend in a strange town.

The pony took a step towards Nicky, then stopped. Nicky knew better than to rush it. It seemed wary, and probably hadn't been handled much before.

Making sure he didn't meet the pony's eye, Nicky turned slightly to the side and stared ahead. The pony watched him, but Nicky kept staring away into the distance. "It's OK, boy," he whispered gently, "take your time. I'm here if you want me."

He'd done this a hundred times before and it never failed. Horses always run from danger – that's how they survive. But Nicky knew they were herd animals too, and they need the safety of numbers. By turning away, he was giving the pony a silent message. He wouldn't hurt it and he wouldn't chase it, but if the pony wanted to come to him – if it wanted to join his "herd" – then he was waiting.

And the pony understood. He took several paces forward, then came up close to Nicky. His nose touched Nicky's shoulder. Nicky took two paces sideways, and the pony followed. He stopped when Nicky stopped. He walked when Nicky walked. Together they walked and stopped, walked and stopped, keeping nose to shoulder across the dusky field.

At the edge of the field Nicky stopped again, and

moved round to face the pony. Reaching up, he rubbed its forehead, then blew a greeting into his face. The pony snorted gently and blew back.

It was a magic moment. However many times it happened to Nicky, it still always made him feel he was touching the stars. He ran his hand along the pony's neck. "So how about it?" he said softly. "Just a quiet walk round your field? Give us both something to do."

The pony didn't flinch as Nicky pressed down on to his back and vaulted on.

Nicky forgot his tiredness. He could live with the blisters and the sores. He remembered now what he was running from. He remembered what he was running to.

As he relaxed into the easy stride of the pony, he thought suddenly how much easier this would be if he could have brought a horse. He began to daydream about Eclipse. He was still missing her. He still ached for her. It was a mad thought, but it would have been great to have done all this with her. Instead she was probably stuck in that stable, or being forced to carry that jerk Edward while his dad waved the whip about at them. A pair of prats, Edward and his dad…

Nicky nudged the chestnut into a sudden gallop, letting the thunder of hooves drown out the memories that began to cloud his mood.

At last he slowed back to a walk, then headed towards the gate. He'd wasted enough time. The chestnut was a gem, but he had to move on.

But when he reached the gate, a new idea hit him. It was crazy and wild, but it could work. And if it worked, it was a way of making certain he got to the fair on time.

Leaning forward to open the latch on the gate, he rode the pony through into the next field. And the next. And the next. And they walked like that together all night, just quietly sharing the dark, and the silence, and the adventure.

15

The birds woke noisily, a chaos of sound across the dawn. Daylight came quickly.

Nicky dismounted, brushed the pony all over with a firm, massaging hand, then set him loose into the next field. He knew he wouldn't come to any harm. There'd be a fuss, and a search, and when the animal was found safe and well the owners would put it down to pranksters, and keep a closer eye on the pony for a week or two. If nothing else happened, something new would come along, and they'd worry about that instead.

Nicky hoped he'd even done the owner a favour. The chestnut was unbroken. He had never been ridden before tonight. But he could be trusted with a baby on his back from now on.

He walked another hour as the sun rose higher, putting a safe distance between himself and the pony.

Later he slept through the heat of the day on a shaded bank by a tiny stream.

He woke in the afternoon, snacked on bread and cold meat, and washed in the clear bubbling water. Then he followed a bridle track to a sleepy village where he bought more drink and food before carrying on across the fields again.

That evening, just as the sun was setting, Nicky searched for, and found, another horse.

It was a thin blue roan with feathered hooves, and she stood apart from the other horses in the field and watched suspiciously as Nicky walked amongst them. When he glanced towards her she laid her ears back, stretched her neck angrily, and stamped her front legs on the ground with warning strikes.

"That's the one," Nicky murmured. "That's the one for tonight."

He looked away again, working his way through the little herd, making friends with each of them. And all the time he was quietly edging nearer to the roan, waiting until she was close enough for him to touch.

When the time was right, Nicky turned to face her, rubbed her forehead, and began scratching the knotty mane. She was a scraggy-looking animal.

Her coat was muddy and rubbed away in places, and her mane and tail were matted. Horses in groups usually groom each other, using gentle bites and nibbles, keeping their companions free of loose hair and rough patches. No one – neither horse nor human – had done that for this mare for a long, long time. "So you're the one on the outside, eh?" Nicky spoke gently as he worked, scraping through the mud and knots with his fingernails. "You're the one that's not in anybody's gang."

It took a long time, scratching off loose hair and dead skin. Checking as he worked, Nicky could see a muddle of colours tinting the mare's neck and forehead – a mix of tired, sludgey greys and browns. They weren't quite part of her, they just hovered around her – like the dull glow of light from a torch with tired batteries. Nicky had seen colours round horses before. He'd been really young the first time it had happened – not more than three or four – and he remembered running excitedly to Grandad, thinking he could see the colours too. Grandad gave him a thoughtful look. Keep that to yourself, he told him. Not everyone has that sort of gift. Not everyone will understand. So Nicky never mentioned it again, not even to Dad, but it helped him a lot over the years when he was working with horses that were sick in some way.

"But you're not sick, old lady," Nicky whispered,

"not in the body anyway. You're just scared, hurt, and very sad."

As he leaned against her, Nicky suddenly felt the response he'd been waiting for. The big, angry mare was licking and smacking her lips, turning her head and nuzzling Nicky like a newborn foal turning trustingly towards its mother.

She stood like a lamb as Nicky pulled himself up on to her, and let him ride her gently through the night. As they walked he talked and sang, and the mare flicked her ears back, listening. By the time the sun rose they were the best of friends, and the muddle of colours had gone.

Nicky set her free in a field full of cows and she followed him to the gate. "I'd keep you with me if I could," he whispered, letting her chew on his sleeve as he hugged her goodbye, "but perhaps now you feel a bit better inside, the world outside will seem a kinder place."

The mare pushed against the gate, whickering to Nicky as he walked away. After a moment she dropped her head slightly, then turned and walked back towards the watching cows. She would stand amongst them, waiting quietly, until the farmer came to check his herd later that morning.

Nicky chose two more horses, riding them through the night until he got close enough to the fair.

Each one was a horse with problems. Each one was a horse who had something he could cure.

He did it as a thank you – to the horse, and to the owner. It was a way of paying for the horse's time, and for any trouble he might have caused. Every horse was different – better – when the owner got it back.

16

The main street was buzzing. On either side were stalls selling everything from bridles to bananas, harnesses to hot dogs. Nicky waved briefly at a toothless old blacksmith, an ancient display of "yesterday's tools" laid out on a bench in front of him. Normally he would have stopped and fingered the old branding irons and rods, but today there wasn't time to waste.

Down the middle of the road horses were being shown off, scattering the crowds as their riders came racing them through.

Nicky didn't stop for any of it. His eyes were fixed on a group of men gathered near the trailers and pick-ups at the top of the hill.

As he reached them, he pushed his way through to the front. In the centre stood a weathered old man in a brown felt hat, running his hands across a wild-eyed skewbald that was backing away and snorting warily. Another, younger man was hanging tight to the halter.

The old man thumbed his nose thoughtfully. "Your horse doesn't look too happy."

"It's only the noise. She'll settle in no time."

"She looks like trouble to me."

"She just needs a bit of work. My six-year-old daughter rode her through town this morning. She went like a dream for her then."

"She looks more like a nightmare now. She's never worth what you're asking."

"So what you offering?"

"I'll give you five hundred."

"Five hundred! That's half what I paid for her. I could get that for her meat."

"Not these days you couldn't." The old man moved round the back of the horse, talking quietly and checking her hooves and legs. The horse stood still, her ears back. "I'll go for six hundred. It could take me weeks to get her right, and even then I might not get a good price back."

"Well, you're getting a bargain. A real bargain." The two men slapped hands and shook on the deal, and the older man took a wad of cash from his back pocket, counted it out for the seller, and took hold of the horse.

As the younger man slipped away, Nicky stepped forward. "You haven't lost your touch then, Grandad."

The old man glanced round. "So there you are," he said, as if Nicky had just popped out to get some drinks. "I'm glad you've shown up. I can use a bit of help today."

Nicky followed him as he led the horse round the back of the trailers. The animal was still strung up and nervy.

"Can you sort her out a bit, lad? I need a break."

Nicky nodded, taking the halter from Grandad, who disappeared into the crowd.

"Easy, girl. Easy." Nicky rubbed the skewbald's forehead, then led her towards an old bath tub that was pulled up under a tap. The horse drank thirstily, and while she drank Nicky ran his hands over her neck and shoulders. She flinched, but she didn't move away. Nicky kept his hands there for a moment, then moved across to touch her flanks, and under her belly. Everywhere he touched her was deliberate. They were the places on her where, through instinct, she would feel most vulnerable. In the wild, big cats will jump on a horse, clawing its back and biting into the top of its neck. Packs of dogs go for the flanks, ripping the flesh just in front of the hind legs. If the

110

skewbald was letting Nicky touch her in those places, he knew she was trusting him.

Lastly Nicky ran his hands down her legs, picking up and examining her feet, the same way that Grandad had done a few minutes before. It was a final check. However skittish a horse seemed, if it trusted him enough to let him touch its legs and hooves – its means of running, and its greatest defence in the wild – it would be easy to work with.

By the time Grandad came back with his pint of beer, Nicky was riding the skewbald, trotting between the trailers using only his legs, and the halter rope, to guide her.

"I got you a coke and a burger."

"Great." Nicky slipped off the skewbald and sat with Grandad on a patch of warm grass. He didn't need to tie the horse up. She just dropped her head and began grazing peacefully beside him.

"So where are the others?"

"I'm on my own."

"Do they know you're here?"

Nicky shrugged. "They might have guessed, I s'pose."

Grandad looked at him thoughtfully. "It's been a bit rough, has it?"

"You could say that."

"So what are you planning?"

Nicky pulled some strands of grass out from

under the wheels of a nearby trailer and began plaiting them together. "I want to stay here. With you, I mean. And when you move on, I want to come with you."

Grandad sighed and stood up slowly, turning his creased, leathery face towards Nicky. It was the first time he'd looked at him properly since Nicky had arrived. "Your dad's only wanting the best for you. He's only trying to keep you safe. Maybe we'll talk about it later."

Nicky nodded reluctantly. He had wanted to get it sorted now.

"Come on." Grandad poured the dregs of his beer away into the grass. "Let's get some money back on this investment."

He nodded towards the skewbald. Nicky sprang back on to her, and the three of them walked together towards the main street.

Within twenty minutes Grandad was selling the horse to a chubby-faced man with a quiet-eyed daughter. Nicky watched as the two men slapped hands to clinch the deal, and the girl flung her arms round the horse's neck. Nicky walked over to her, sharing her excitement. "She'll go great for you, I can see that."

"Really?" The girl's eyes were shining now. "She's so beautiful. I can't believe she's mine."

"Stand square in front of her, and rub her

forehead." said Nicky. "It'll work like magic. It's a way of gaining her trust – she can't see you from there, so she has to really believe that you won't hurt her."

"I would never hurt her anyway."

"But she doesn't know that yet. Close your eyes."

The girl looked at him shyly, then giggled nervously.

"Go on," said Nicky. "Just for a minute. Keep them shut until I tell you to open them again."

With another giggle the girl did as she was told, looking tense and awkward as she faced Nicky.

"OK. You can open them again now. How did that feel?"

"I felt … scared."

"That's because you couldn't see me, and you couldn't guess what I was going to do. It's the same for horses – especially with strangers." He reached up to touch the skewbald's forehead again, "The more times you touch her here, the quicker she'll learn to feel safe with you. It'll make everything you do with her loads casicr."

The girl gave Nicky an uncertain smile, then stood head on to the horse. Lifting her hand, she rubbed a tentative circle on to the brown and white forehead.

The horse stood stock still for a moment, then nudged her gently, blowing softly into the girl's hair.

"See?" Nicky grinned with delight. "Groom her a lot too, and when you talk to her, don't pat her. Sort of finger-nibble her mane. Like this..." Nicky bent his thumb and finger, and showed her how to work her hand up and down through the mane. "She'll be your best mate, and she'll do anything to please you if you learn how to talk to her properly."

The girl's dad came over. "Right. The deal's all done. Are you ready?"

"Thanks." The girl nodded, then gave Nicky a warm smile before she turned and led the pony away.

Grandad pressed fifty pounds cash into Nicky's hand.

"Your share of the profit," he grunted.

They walked together towards a scowling woman who was trying to offer a thin-faced black pony to a young family. The pony had planted its legs firmly on the ground, its ears were back and its tail swished irritably. However much the woman tugged at it, it wouldn't budge. The father gave a short shake of his head and walked away.

Grandad strolled over and thumbed his nose thoughtfully. "Your horse doesn't look too happy..."

17

"Nicky!"
    "Hey there!"
    "It's great to see you!"
    Karl, Lisa and Beck – all cousins he'd lived with at Beech Forest from time to time – came over as Nicky and Grandad walked back to the trailer that evening. They slapped hands in greeting, and grinned awkwardly at each other.
    "Are you coming to the fair?" Lisa nudged him. "It's getting late. The rides will be getting faster by now."
    They all accepted him being there, and being back in with them, without any questions or need for explanations.
    Nicky walked with them towards the throbbing

music and flashing lights which whirled and wailed in the next field. They did this every year. A hard day selling horses, or tack, or whittling wood for tourists, and then staying out till the early hours, screaming the night away on the Wheel of Torture or the Death Blitzer.

Nicky jostled along with them, joining in the loud, bright banter that they always used.

But after a while he got fed up. The rattling car rides seemed loud and cheap. The music and the lights and the endless screaming was getting to him.

"Coming to the arcade?" Karl thumped him on the back. "Let's lose some of this cash we made today."

"Maybe you could win me a cuddly monster from that claw thing." Lisa brushed up against Nicky, taking his arm in hers.

But suddenly Nicky couldn't be bothered. It all seemed empty and pointless, and he didn't feel part of it. It was as if he was on the outside, watching it all through a sheet of glass.

"No thanks. I've got stuff I need to do." He took Lisa's arm away from his gently, gave them all a quick smile, and walked away.

They looked at each other, shrugged, then moved on, disappearing into the throng and bustle of the fairground.

* * *

Nicky went back amongst the trailers. A few dogs watched him suspiciously, but other than that the field was deserted. Most people were either at the funfair, or down at the pubs in the main street.

He walked back to Grandad's trailer and slumped against the wheel. It was dark now, and he stared up at the star-peppered sky. The restlessness, the ache for something he couldn't name, was still with him. Coming here hadn't made it go away.

"You look a bit distant, boy. Are you anywhere good?"

Nicky started as Grandad came up beside him. "You don't usually roll home till the early hours on fair night. What are you doing back?"

"I could ask you the same question."

Grandad sat with him outside the trailer. His old Lurcher, Penny, plonked herself between them.

Nicky scratched the big dog's ears absently, then turned to Grandad. "So what did you and Dad fall out about?"

Grandad sighed. "I guessed that was coming."

"Well?"

Grandad rolled himself a cigarette. "It was about you."

"Me?" Nicky turned to him. "What the hell were you fighting about me for?"

"Because of your gift. Because of what you can do."

"With horses, you mean?"

Grandad was quiet for a long time. "You know about Ellie, don't you?"

"A bit."

"D'you know what happened?"

"Only that there was a terrible accident. Dad never talks about it."

"None of us ever do. Maybe that's been the problem." Grandad sighed again. "But your dad was there watching. He saw it happen. The horse went wild, completely mad. It – it was a nightmare for him."

"Do you ever think about Ellie?"

"Sometimes I get flashes of her. I think about what she'd be like now. Who she might be married to…"

Nicky looked out into the darkness, suddenly seeing a vision of Ellie – dark hair, dark eyes, probably someone a bit like Dad. And the night air seemed thick with the ghosts of children who had never been born. Cousins he had never had.

"Anyway," Grandad let his breath out in a slow whistle, "she's long gone now. It's best left buried. The past can weigh you down for ever, if you let it."

Nicky nodded. You could go nuts, thinking about what might have been. And you still wouldn't be able to change anything. He pulled his thoughts back round to the present. "But I still don't see what all that's got to do with me."

"Ellie was like you, Nicky. She had the gift. She could talk to horses. It was as if she could do magic with them. They'd do anything for her. And your dad worshipped Ellie. He changed a lot after the accident."

"In what way?"

"He'd been a bright lad. Cheeky. Lively. Always getting into scraps and stuff. Always on the go. He used to ride a lot too. He was good with horses then."

"Dad used to ride?" Nicky was stunned. "He's never said. I thought he was just not interested in horses."

"Only once Ellie was gone. He just seemed to close down about everything after that. He was off on his own a lot. He went moody and difficult, and got in trouble with the gavvers. We just couldn't get close to him any more. It was only Kathleen – your mum – that he would even tolerate anywhere near him. She was just a scrap of a girl then, of course, but she was his only friend."

Nicky was quiet. A couple stumbled past nearby. Somewhere in the background a dog barked. Thin wisps of music drifted across from the fairground.

"But why did Dad suddenly start to mind about me and horses? Even if he had something against them himself, he always used to let me work with you. Why did he change?"

"It was that horse. The mad one. The one with the tumour. When he heard you'd been bitten, he just seemed to flip. It was as if all the fear he'd been trying to push back came flooding out. And he was wild with me. He thought I'd taken a risk, letting you work with that horse – he thought I'd let you walk into danger."

"But I wanted to go with you that day. And anyway, I have to be with horses wherever I am. I'd go mad otherwise."

"I know that, Nicky. That was what I told him that night. I thought what you had was so special, so wonderful, and what happened to Ellie shouldn't hold you down. I wouldn't agree to stop taking you with me."

"So is that when he made us all leave?"

"Yep. I went off that night – I couldn't stand to listen to him any more. But I didn't really think he'd go. A Gypsy doesn't pull up his roots like that. Not normally."

"Dad's not normal about lots of things now."

Grandad sighed. "Maybe he hasn't been for a long time."

Nicky sat in silence, his hands on his knees, thinking about Dad. If he was honest, Dad had always been different. He kept himself apart. He did things his own way, even if it caused trouble.

He always seemed cut off from the main group, even when they lived amongst them. Nicky tried to imagine how he'd feel if something terrible suddenly happened to Sabrina. Would he be like Dad? Would he carry it with him all his life, letting it shadow everything he did? Wouldn't that just mean two lives were destroyed, instead of one? "So what happens now?" he said at last.

"You belong with your dad. He's doing his best. I suppose that's all any of us can ever do."

Nicky stared out across the endless night.

Nearby a fight broke out, two drunks sprawling and cursing on the ground.

In the trailer opposite someone else the worse for drink was being sick.

"It's rotten living there though. I hate it."

"It's not great anywhere these days," Grandad said gently. "Remember all those gavver raids. Always moving on. Always being blamed. Times are changing for us Gypsies. There's less and less places to go. I suppose your dad's trying to make something new for you all."

"Do you think he's right?"

Grandad shrugged. "There's no such thing as right and wrong, Nicky. Nothing's ever that black and white. There's only ways of looking at things, and deciding which paths to follow."

"There's other stuff too though," Nicky began.

"There's this jerk at school. His name's Edward, and he's been giving me a hard time, saying I've been hurting horses."

"And have you?"

"Of course not!"

"So what's your problem? As long as *you* know you're clean, you can hold your head up."

"I do, but he just keeps on and on. And he gets other people in on it too."

"So what's his problem?"

"What do you mean?"

"Why is he doing it? Why does he hate you that much? It takes a lot of energy to hate someone. There must be something about you – a jealousy, or maybe a fear."

Nicky shrugged. "He's clever. He's rich. He's popular. I haven't got anything he'd want."

Grandad rolled himself another cigarette. "Well, you might never find out, but you just have to keep above it. There's no point trying to run from him. There's an Edward in every town, especially when you're a Gypsy."

Nicky hesitated, wondering if he should tell Grandad about Eclipse, and the paint spraying, and everything that was happening. Out of all the people in the world, Grandad was probably the only one who would really understand. "He's got this horse…"

* * *

"We've had a great time. You should have stayed." Lisa burst upon them, grinning and giggling and clutching a cuddly panda. Beck was just behind her. Nicky turned to look at them. "Where's Karl?"

"He's gone to his trailer. He got in a fight with some New Age Travellers, and got a bloody nose. You know what it's like."

Nicky nodded. He'd forgotten, but he was remembering now. Grandad was right. It could be good here, but it could be grotty too.

Probably nowhere was ever that great. Not all of the time.

"I'm turning in now." Grandad turned to him. "You coming?"

Nicky nodded and followed him into the trailer.

He lay in the bunk and listened to the night-long noises of the fair. The laughing. The shouting. The screaming.

And he thought about Dad, and Mum, and Sabrina.

In the morning, he let Grandad drive him home.

18

"**S**o you're back." Dad crawled out from under the pick-up, and gave a brief nod as Nicky and Grandad walked towards him. His hands were greasy, and he picked up a dirty red rag from his pocket and began wiping them slowly, as if clean fingers were the most important thing in the world at a time like this.

Nobody spoke.

Nicky took a deep breath. "I – I'm sorry, Dad."

Dad threw the rag away suddenly, and stared at him.

Nicky pushed his hands deep into his pockets. He hadn't expected balloons and banners, but Dad wasn't even meeting him halfway. He stared back, their eyes locking together like bull's horns.

It was Dad who broke first. "So what have you got to say for yourself?"

"Like I said, I'm sorry."

Dad snorted. "You'd better tell that to your mum. She's the one who's been gazing out of windows hoping you'd suddenly spring up out of fresh air, and giving herself a hard time about where she went wrong with you. I suppose you didn't think of what she might be going through."

"I—"

"I knew he'd go running to you." Dad turned on Grandad suddenly.

"At least he had the sense to go somewhere he'd be safe." Grandad didn't flinch from Dad's glare.

At that moment there was a shout from the trailer and Mum came racing out. She took Nicky's hands and twirled him round. She hugged him. She thumped him on the chest with her fists. She hugged him again, and then burst into tears.

Nicky hugged her back awkwardly. Perhaps he preferred Dad's reaction after all. "I'm all right, Mum. You knew I'd be all right."

"Do you think that stopped us worrying?" Mum thumped him once more, but it was softer this time. She looked across at Dad and Grandad. "Come inside. I'll make a pot of tea, and we'll save the row till later."

Grandad shook his head. "Me and Joseph have got some talking to do."

"Too right."

Nicky saw that Dad had his fists clenched. He was breathing hard, the veins standing out on his forehead. Surely he wouldn't punch Grandad? He gave Mum an anxious glance.

"Leave them," whispered Mum, catching his eye. And putting her hand on Nicky's shoulder, she steered him past Sky, who was jumping and pulling at her rope with delight, and into the trailer.

They sat in the kitchen while Mum boiled the kettle.

"Do you think they'll be all right?" Nicky looked out of the window. Dad and Grandad were walking away across the site. They weren't talking, and even their backs looked stiff and angry.

"In the end," Mum sighed. "Once they've fought it all out."

"I know about Ellie. I know what it did to Dad, after the accident."

Mum nodded. "He's never got over it. It still haunts him now. I don't blame him, I know what he went through…" Her voice trailed off, then she added, "But I'm sorry about the way it's been passed on to you. No one should have to live their lives with a ghost from the past hanging over them."

Nicky got one last glance of Dad and Grandad before they disappeared from view. He didn't say anything, but he reckoned they'd be gone a long time.

He went into Jim's trailer to shower and change.

Jim, who was dozing in the corner, woke up. "Good to see you." His voice was lazy, unhurried.

Nicky went to his rucksack and pulled out the fifty pounds he and Grandad had made on the skewbald. He handed it to Jim. "I don't think Dad feels it's that good."

Jim sat up, pulling his braces up over his shoulders. He took the wad of notes from Nicky, got the empty cereal packet out from the back of the kitchen cabinet, and put the notes back in the tin. He didn't ask any questions. "Don't be hard on your dad," he said suddenly. "He wants the best for you."

"Maybe." Nicky looked at him for a moment. Jim was much older than Dad, but he'd still been around when Dad was a boy. "Did you know Ellie very well?" he said suddenly.

Jim laughed. "I used to look after her when she was just a scrap of a kid. Watched her grow up. Her and your dad."

"What was she like?"

"Pretty. Funny. Lots of charm. She could twist your dad round her little finger. He'd have done anything for her."

"Was she much like Dad?"

Jim stared at Nicky for a moment, then shook his head slowly. "She was more like you. Not just the gift with horses, but the way you act, and the way

127

you think. Sometimes, when I listen to you talking, it almost seems like—"

There was a knock on the door and Mum came in. "I've done spaghetti and meatballs next door. I thought you might be hungry."

"Thanks." Nicky nodded at Jim, who was stretching and yawning. "Are you coming over later? Grandad's here at the moment."

"Fine. I'll get a fire going for this evening. We can have a few beers and dream about old times together." Jim yawned again, and Nicky got up and followed Mum next door.

A few minutes later he was ploughing his way through a mountain of spaghetti and meatballs.

He'd just started on a giant slice of treacle pudding, when he saw Dad and Grandad through the window. Dad was showing Grandad something, and Grandad was nodding. "I can't see any blood," he whispered to Mum.

She leaned over Nicky's shoulder. "I think Dad might have even laughed then."

"Probably a trick of the light," said Nicky. But he shot Mum a quick look, and they both smiled.

A few minutes later Dad and Grandad came in.

They drank coffee and grumbled about gorgios, and money, and the site manager at Beech Forest. Nicky listened quietly. It was great, hearing them growling away together. Almost like old times. He felt light and easy, like something heavy was being lifted away from him.

Suddenly Dad put his mug down with a clatter, and turned to Nicky. "Come and give me a hand with the pick-up a minute. I need you to get a new wheel on while I jack it up."

Leaving Grandad and Mum, Nicky followed Dad outside. Dad set up the jack while Nicky loosened the wheel nuts. The pick-up rose slowly into the air. "I've been talking to Grandad," he grunted at last. "I don't agree with everything he said, but ... some of it ... well, some of what's been wrong ... I admit I've added to it."

Nicky slipped off the old wheel, and swopped it with the spare. "I wouldn't have run if I hadn't hated it here."

"I knew that. I knew that."

"And I never hurt those horses. I never would."

"I knew that too. The gavvers came over to have a word with me, and confirm they were finished with you. And that woman – the one from Badger Farm – isn't going to do anything about your trespassing on her land." Dad gave a dry laugh. "She must have known she wouldn't get much out of us anyway. But ... Grandad said you were asking about Ellie."

"A bit."

"She was just your age when it happened."

"I know." Nicky waited, half-terrified and half-relieved that Dad was talking to him about it at last. The whole world seemed to hold its breath as he bent and tightened the wheel nuts.

Dad dropped the jack back down again suddenly. "I was there, with her. I should have done something…"

Something in his voice made Nicky look up, and his heart twisted. Dad's face looked strange, lost, and helpless. As if he was hardly more than a boy himself.

"I – I'm sorry," Nicky said. He couldn't think of what else to say. But Dad's expression scared him. Grandad was right. Sometimes things were best left buried.

"I'm sorry too." Dad's voice was still wavering. He closed his eyes, as if he was blotting out the past. Shutting it away again. There was a long silence. When he spoke next he had his old voice back. Gentler. Warmer. But still the voice Nicky knew. "Look – I know this life we're living here feels hard, but worse things could happen. And if there was a real disaster, you'd look back on all this as if it was a picnic. You might even long for it."

Nicky looked round him. There were still logs everywhere. Old tyres grown over with weeds. A rusty supermarket trolley. It was hard to imagine ever longing for this. But he glanced back at Dad and nodded. "Maybe you're right."

Dad punched him lightly on the arm – a friendly gesture, something he hadn't done for years. "You just have to take what you can from each day. You never know what's coming next…"

There was a sudden shriek, and Sabrina came whirling round the corner. She flung herself at Nicky, squeezing him tight. "I thought I'd never see you again!"

"Well, you were unlucky." Nicky grinned, disentangling himself from her. "You don't get rid of me that easily."

Dad chucked the punctured wheel into the back of the pick-up. "I'm going inside. I'll see you two in a minute."

Sabrina tucked her arm into Nicky's, talking breathlessly. "It's been miserable without you. Mum kept crying, and Dad pretended he wasn't bothered, but he kept watching out the window, and going outside if Sky ever barked and stuff like that. I wasn't scared for you though. I knew you'd look out for yourself. I saw Grandad's trailer just now. Did you go to the fair?"

"Yep." Nicky let her warm chatter flow over him, welcoming and safe.

"Lucky you. I wish I could've gone, instead of being stuck behind the bars of that classroom…"

Her words jarred into him, the mention of school like a trap springing shut. He spoke carefully, his voice suddenly tight. "Has anyone there said anything about me?"

"They've said loads. Mostly the usual stuff – you know, like you've gone off to join a circus, or you've stolen a racehorse, or you've stowed away on a boat to Ireland."

"Does anyone know what really happened?"

"Only that girl. The thin one with the pretty eyes. She's been asking about you every day."

"I bet she has," Nicky muttered, the old aching pain suddenly crushing him. If Bretta was asking about him, it must be so she could pass it on to Edward.

The police might have let him go, but as far as Bretta and Edward were concerned, he would always be guilty, and there wasn't anything he could ever do about it.

19

It happened the next evening.

It was Friday, and Mum let Nicky stay home "just to finish off the week".

But it wasn't all that great, staying off. He spent the day knocking on doors with Dad and Jim, looking for logging work in the next town. Most people were polite – those that bothered to listen to them in the first place. But they had a couple of doors slammed in their faces, and one old woman chased them down the path with a broom.

They gave up early and went back to the pitch, where Dad and Jim spent the time tinkering with the pick-ups.

Time moved slowly. Nicky mooched about,

kicking around by the garages and flicking aimlessly through the dull afternoon telly programmes.

Grandad had gone off straight after breakfast. The horse fair was over, and he was joining some of the others, then heading on up to Wales. As Nicky watched his old white pick-up bump away across the site, the ache in him grew. Things here weren't really any better. Dad seemed brighter – not exactly cheerful, but Nicky noticed he at least looked at him now when he spoke. But it wasn't that. It was horses. He and Dad still hadn't talked about horses.

"Pub night tonight," Dad said, after Sabrina came home from school.

"I want an early night." Now it was Nicky who wouldn't meet Dad's eyes.

"Maybe we should all stay home," Mum suggested.

"I've got school work anyway. If I do it now, it gets it out of the way for the rest of the week-end."

"Mind you stay inside then," said Dad. "Your grandad thinks I should trust you more, so I'm taking a chance. Don't let me down."

"Why would I?" Nicky made his voice sound hurt as he flicked over to the next channel. "I'm going to get myself something to eat, get this work done, then get to bed." It was the truth. Dad needn't worry. Nicky really was shattered, and he was staying in tonight even if Eclipse herself came knocking on the door.

As the others drove away he leaned his head on the back of the seat, and let himself drift.

It was Sky's frantic barking that roused him. Nicky looked outside but he couldn't see anything. Still, Sky was definitely upset about something. Her fur was all up, and she was growling low in her throat as she strained against the rope.

Maybe it was a fox, or even a badger, sniffing round the rubbish bags. They did that a lot, tearing at the plastic and strewing all the cans and boxes and mouldy bits of vegetables everywhere. It was a disgusting job clearing it all up. Nicky stepped outside to check round the back of the trailer, ready to chase whatever it was away.

"Going for your evening stroll?"

Sky's bark became a wild frenzy, but her warning was too late.

Nicky was punched, then grabbed on either side, his arms twisted and locked behind him.

Gasping, he glared up at his attackers. Liam and Matt. He should have guessed.

"What the hell … what you doing … get off me!" Nicky struggled. He was strong and he could always handle himself, but the others were bigger and the punch had winded him.

"What you gonna do, Gyppo? Put a curse on us?" Matt twisted his grip on Nicky's arm. Nicky swore quietly, but he didn't cry out.

They dragged him, pulling him away from the trailer towards the garages, and then down the side road which led round the back of some boarded-up shops.

Nicky knew suddenly where they were taking him – they were heading for the old scout hut, a tumble-down building hidden from the road by a tangle of hedges and trees.

So now he knew where. He just didn't know why.

But as they turned the corner and Nicky saw the thin grey curl of smoke that wound upwards from a clearing in the bushes, he guessed it wasn't likely that they were inviting him to a barbecue.

20

"What do you want?" Nicky wasn't bothering to struggle against them. Their grip was too strong. He would have to play for time. Pretend he was going to go along with whatever it was they were planning.

"We warned you, didn't we? We told you to leave off the horses, but you can't seem to stop yourself. You did another one last Friday, and another one on Saturday, after everyone thought you'd done a runner. You must've been hanging around, keeping low."

As they pushed through into the clearing, the fire was burning well. It cracked and snapped, spitting angry orange sparks into the air.

"We've built this in your honour, Gyppo. We thought you might like to dance round it."

"Or if you're hungry, we reckoned you could even snack on a few flames. We've heard your sort can do all kinds of weirdo tricks."

Liam fixed a firmer grip on Nicky's arms, and Matt pulled a length of string from his pocket. He began twisting it round Nicky's ankles, tying them together. This time Nicky did struggle, but Liam had his arms locked hard behind him, and it was no good.

Suddenly there was a movement to his left. Looking round, Nicky saw Edward Carter swinging towards him. Behind him, looking pale and scared and smaller than ever, trotted Billy Clarke.

"It's good to have you back, Nicky. We missed you in school." Edward stopped just behind the fire.

"I might have known you'd have set this up. A jerk like you wouldn't be able to manage anything on your own." Nicky spoke hoarsely, his face drained of colour.

Edward laughed. "Watch the insults, Gyppo. We're going to teach you a little lesson, that's all. Horses mean a lot to us, and we don't like seeing them get hurt."

Nicky saw, for the first time, that Billy was holding something. A metal rod. He knew straight away what it was. It was a branding iron – like the ones the old blacksmith always put out at the fair.

He raised his eyes from the rod to Billy. Billy wouldn't look at him.

138

"Billy made you a little present. Something to help you with your alphabet." Edward laughed again. "Put your hand up Gyppo. Tell teacher if you recognize the shape on the end." Edward lifted the tip of the rod which was trailing in the grass. It was a rough piece of forging, and the corners were more round than bent, but there was no mistaking what it was. The metal shape on the end had been heated then bent to make a letter "N".

Nicky swallowed hard, and a rush of bile rose in his throat.

"You look a bit shaky, Gyppo. What are you worried about?" Edward's face was very close. His voice dropped slightly. "We're only going to do to you what you do to the horses. Come on, Billy. Heat it up."

"I … I … it'll burn him."

"That's the idea, stupid. Now get on with it. I'd do it myself, only I can't with these crutches."

Nicky's throat tightened as Billy pushed the tip of the rod into the fire. He could see the letter "N" begin to glow as the heat spread through it. Where would they put it? On his hands? On his face?

"Get his shirt off. We'll do it on his back." Edward's eyes narrowed suddenly. "See how good I am to you, Gyppo. No one will ever see it. Not unless you get hot shifting brick rubble or something, and decide to strip off to the waist one day."

Nicky felt a sharp twist of pain as Liam bent his arm back behind him, and Matt began to tear at his sleeve. "Get off me!" Fear seemed to whistle through him, stinging and screaming under his skin. "GET OFF ME!"

"What the hell do you all think you're doing!"

Billy jumped backwards, dropping the rod with a childish squeal.

The others froze.

Bretta Miles, her face screwed up with horror, was running towards them.

For a moment, nobody spoke.

"I – I didn't think we were really going to do it. Edward s-s-s-said it would just be a j-j-j-joke."

Bretta glanced at Edward, then back at Billy. "I saw you all in a huddle in the school field at lunch time. Was this what you were planning?"

Liam exchanged glances with Matt. "We were only giving him a taste of his own medicine."

"And Billy's right," Edward sounded irritated. "We weren't really going to go through with it. We're not stupid. We just wanted to frighten him enough to stop him hurting horses like he does."

"I don't hurt horses! I don't care what you call me, or what you think. I DON'T HURT HORSES!"

"Untie him." Bretta turned to Liam, and her voice was like ice.

Liam nodded at Matt, and his brother pulled a penknife from his pocket and sliced through the string.

Nicky jerked himself free from Liam, pushed roughly past Edward and Billy, and walked away.

He wasn't going to give any of them the satisfaction of seeing him run.

21

"Nicky!"

Nicky sat in the trailer, his head buried in his hands. He hadn't stopped shaking since he got inside.

"Nicky, it's Bretta. Please open the door. I need to speak to you."

Nicky kept as still as stone. After a while she stopped hammering, and he heard her footsteps squelch away across the site.

He was glad.

He didn't want to talk to Bretta.

He didn't want to talk to anyone.

And he especially didn't want anyone to see that he'd been crying.

22

"What's up?"

"Nothing." Nicky was helping Dad fix the electrics on the pick-up, and he kept his head down under the bonnet.

"You've had a face like sour cheese since you got up this morning. If you're sulking because I wouldn't let you go back with Grandad—"

"I'm not sulking."

"We're a family, Nicky. We should stick together, whatever happens."

"I *said* I'm not sulking. Now leave off, OK?" Nicky couldn't tell him. He would never tell anyone what had happened last night with Edward and his mob. But he'd never forget it either. It was stuck in his head, and every time he thought about it, he felt a flood of shame. The way they'd caught him. The way they'd pushed him around. Part of him even wished Bretta hadn't come along when she did. It didn't feel that brilliant to have been saved by her either.

"Nicky!" Reluctantly he looked round at the sound of Sabrina's voice. She'd been out with Mum, like she did every Saturday morning, selling peat that they'd bagged up from the farms nearby.

"What do you want?"

"I just saw that girl again. The one from school. She was hanging around at the end of the road."

"So?"

"She came up to me. She looked all worried and upset. And she wanted to ask if you'd go round to her house."

"To her *house*!" Nicky straightened up fully and turned to stare at Sabrina. He'd never been to anyone's house before in his life. "Why?"

"I dunno." Sabrina shrugged. "She gave me this map. It shows you how to get there." She pulled a chocolate wrapper from her pocket with a felt-penned diagram scribbled on the back. "She said to tell you it was urgent. She said she was going back home to wait for you there."

She handed the scrumpled paper to Nicky and watched him for a moment as he looked at it. Then she grinned suddenly. "I reckon she fancies you."

"Get lost!" Nicky felt the colour rise to his face as he shoved the wrapper into his jeans pocket.

"Have you finished that yet?" Dad stuck his head out the window of the pick-up. "I'm ready to try and start her up."

"Nearly." Nicky leaned back inside the bonnet again and tightened the bolts. But his mind was only half on the job.

What did Bretta Miles want with him now?

23

The shrill ring of the bell buzzed deep inside the house.

Nicky saw a blurred shape appear behind the dappled glass of the front door. He wanted to run, but there wasn't time.

"Thanks for coming." It was Bretta who appeared.

"Sabrina said it was important." Nicky stared down at the polished red tiles of the doorstep.

"I've got to talk to you. I was coming to see you yesterday when—"

"I don't want to talk about yesterday."

Bretta hesitated. "Do you want to come in?"

"No." Nicky felt his skin begin to prickle. The narrow hall behind her, and the smell of the carpet, were getting to him.

Bretta pulled a denim jacket from a hook on the wall. "We'll go for a walk then. I've got to pick up the paper for Mum anyway."

She stepped outside and they walked together towards the newsagent's.

For a while neither of them spoke, then Bretta glanced at Nicky. "I want to say sorry again."

Nicky didn't answer. He was sick of her blaming him all the time. "I know I didn't do anything. You can think what you like."

"Please, Nicky. I feel really rough about it. If I could take it all back, I would. Even yesterday was partly my fault."

"How's that?" His voice thickened. He'd already told her he wanted to forget yesterday.

"Something I said to Edward, after the police caught you last week. I told him I wished someone would frighten you one day, the way you frighten horses. He must have thought I meant it."

Nicky's face set like stone. If she'd asked him to come out here so she could ease her conscience, she could think again. "I *don't* frighten horses!"

Bretta sighed. "I know you don't."

"You've said that before."

"But this time I really know. This time I'm really sure."

"Why?"

"It was your sister Sabrina that started me off.

She was crying at school last Friday, and she told me you'd disappeared." Bretta wound a strand of hair round her finger as she talked. "I felt sort of guilty about that too. I knew you'd gone partly because of me. It was me that followed you that night. It was me that got the police out. I hated doing it because … well, whenever I talk to you, you don't *seem* as if you'd hurt horses. You don't *seem* as if you'd hurt anything. So I was really upset that Edward kept on being right."

Nicky shrugged. "So what's changed? As far as you're concerned, I was still caught red-handed."

Bretta took a deep breath. "When Sabrina told me you'd run off, she made me promise not to tell anyone you'd gone. She said it would only mean the kids in her class would have something new to rib her about. So I didn't mention it, not even to Edward. I didn't say anything till Monday, and that was only because everyone knew by then. Your dad came round, calling on people, looking for you."

"So?"

"On Saturday night another horse was sprayed. It was in a field near Billy's house. Edward rang me to tell me, going on and on about how even the police catching you hadn't sorted you out. But you must have been long gone by then."

"Well maybe I was just hiding in the bushes all the time. Us Gypsies are good at that."

"I did think that might have happened – except for two things. First, Sabrina told me yesterday that you'd been at that horse fair. That's over a hundred kilometres away. If you were still hanging round here on Saturday, I don't reckon you'd have made it—"

"I might have done. If I'd hitched a lift." Nicky wasn't about to make this easy for her.

"Then my friend Zoë rang me at the weekend. She used to go to school here, but they moved to a village about fifteen kilometres away last year. She was in a right state because her pony had been stolen."

Nicky laughed suddenly. "Oh, so that makes sense. I must have been too busy stealing *her* pony to have been here spraying graffiti on anyone else's."

Bretta bit her lip, and went on. "He was a young pony. Unbroken. And they'd been having trouble with him. He was a bit wild. A bit ... stroppy."

Nicky looked straight ahead, suddenly remembering the chestnut with the white blaze and four white stockings. "So how come you think I took it?"

"I didn't at first. It didn't enter my head. But Zoë rang me yesterday to say that they'd found him, just left in a field about twenty kilometres from where he'd been taken. And she said it was really weird ... the pony was different. As quiet as a lamb. She's going to try putting a saddle on him next weekend… Nicky?"

"What?"

"If she does try to put a saddle on him, do you think he'll still be stroppy?"

Nicky was quiet for a moment, then he turned and met Bretta full in the eye. "I think she'll find he's just fine from now on."

Bretta met the look, and nodded slowly. "That's what I thought you'd say."

They reached the newsagent's. Nicky hung back from the door. "So is that it then? Is that everything you wanted to say?"

"No. There's something else. It's to do with Eclipse. She's been a bit funny lately."

Nicky felt something twist in his chest. "Is she ill?"

"I don't think so. It's just more of a restlessness really. But I need you to come to the stables with me and have a look. Edward's dad's away at the moment, and Edward said he was going out tonight. We could go over there this evening and…"

Nicky shook his head. "My dad will do his nut if I get caught round another horse at the moment. Things have settled down a bit at home, but it could all explode again if I do anything crazy."

"OK." Bretta nodded. "Maybe I'll pop over on my own, after tea. It's probably nothing anyway.

They've got that show-jumping trial next week, so she might just be picking up on tension about that. Apparently the Olympic selectors are going to be there, picking out the best riders. I know Edward's really twitchy about it."

"I'm not surprised," said Nicky, remembering how pathetic he was in the School last week. Edward didn't look like he was going to be ready to walk along the beach on a donkey, let alone put himself up for some top-class show-jumping team.

"Anyway, thanks for coming out," Bretta smiled at him. "I've got to go now, otherwise I'll get it in the neck from Mum. I'll see you around."

"Yeah. Sure." Nicky stood for a moment as she disappeared inside the shop, then turned and walked thoughtfully home.

24

Nicky waited till after tea, when Dad and Jim had gone to clear someone's garden. "I need to go out."

"Where to?" Mum was washing the dishes, while Sabrina wiped.

"To see a mate. About my homework."

Sabrina nudged Mum. "He's got a girlfriend. Someone from school."

Mum raised her eyebrows. "A gorgio friend? Are you sure she's all right?"

"She's fine." Nicky glared at Sabrina, who was grinning and winking.

"Well, be careful then," Mum said at last. "And don't let her drag you into any trouble."

Nicky grabbed his jacket, unlocked his bike from

the trailer tow bar, and cycled off. He had to go. He couldn't keep away. Not now Bretta had said there was something wrong with Eclipse. He knew what people like Declan Carter were capable of, especially before a big event. If Eclipse was getting nervy, it might mean they were doing things to her, trying to hype her up to make her perform better. And the Declan Carters of this world usually did that through fear rather than kindness.

He saw the car as soon as he arrived – Declan Carter's black Porsche, parked up on the verge near the gate.

Nicky hesitated. He was taking a big chance hanging around here if Declan Carter was about. Bretta thought he was away, but perhaps he had come back early.

Nicky crouched behind the bushes for a moment, listening. Dusk was falling, and a silence hung over the field. The whole place seemed to be holding its breath.

Suddenly he made up his mind. He'd have to take the risk. If Declan Carter really was putting pressure on Eclipse, this was a chance to find out.

The silence grew as Nicky crept into the field. There were no birds calling. No small scuttering animals scampering out of his way. A twig cracked, and it sounded like a pistol shot.

And there was a feeling too. A strange, uneasy feeling. As if there was something very wrong. It was oddly familiar, but Nicky couldn't place it.

The light was fading fast, and the shadows in the field grew dark and dense.

As Nicky slipped between the trees and bushes he made the soft call in his throat that Eclipse always recognized, but she didn't come.

Maybe Edward's dad had her in the school, or in the stable. Nicky was about to slip across and check when a sound reached him. It was muffled and distant, a strange mix between a scuffle and a scream.

In the far corner of the field there was a small copse. Trees and bushes grew tightly together, their branches weaving and tangling. Nicky hadn't paid it much attention because he knew it wasn't somewhere Eclipse would choose to go. Now, still keeping to the shadows, he edged towards it.

As he got nearer the uneasy feeling grew.

Suddenly Nicky knew when he had felt like that before. It was that terrible night at Badger Farm. The night he found the stone-grey pony hobbled and sprayed.

For the first time in his life Nicky forgot about staying hidden. He sprinted madly across the centre of the field towards the copse.

Bursting through a gap in the bushes, he saw

Eclipse. Her head was thrown back in terror, and her eyes glowed wild with fear. All around her, a sense of menace seemed to crackle like sparks of electricity.

And standing facing her, a spray can in his hand, was Edward.

25

Nicky didn't stop to think. As the dark shape of Eclipse tried to stumble away, pressing deeper into the shadows, he launched himself at Edward.

"What the—" Edward spluttered and struggled.

"You creep!" Nicky spat through gritted teeth. "You ugly, vicious, pathetic, bullying creep!"

With the advantage of surprise on his side, he wrestled Edward to the ground.

"Get off me!" Edward twisted, managing to roll sideways, and kicked out.

It was a hard kick, harder than Nicky had expected. Even as he battled to force Edward back down, he knew something was odd. Something was different. It struck him suddenly, like an axe splitting open the heart of a tree. When Nicky had seen him just now, Edward wasn't on crutches. He had been standing perfectly normally.

Edward writhed and kicked again. Struggling to hold him, another image flashed into Nicky's head. It was the image of Edward up by the house, illuminated by lightning that night of the storm. It was the image that had nagged and nagged at his mind when he first ran away. Edward hadn't been on crutches then either. He hadn't even been limping.

Fresh anger burned through him. "Your dad was right!" Nicky's grip bit deep into Edward's shoulders. "You used your leg as an excuse because you were too scared to ride. You thought it would stop you from having to train. Except it didn't work. Your dad wouldn't care if you died in the saddle, as long as you made the Olympic team first. So you came out here in desperation, planning to damage your own horse—"

"Just try and prove it, Gyppo! I might have heard a strange noise. I might have come out to check. You'd better leave off me. My dad will be out here in a minute, and if he finds you near that horse..."

For a moment Nicky hesitated, remembering the Porsche parked up by the gate. Then another thought jarred through him, making him wrench harder. "Don't waste your breath. Your dad's gone away. That's the way you've always done it, isn't it?

157

That's the way you've been out in the night, hurting horses."

"So we're not that different, are we, Gyppo?" Edward stopped struggling, and his voice became wheedling. "You creeping out at night to ride my horse. Me creeping out to drive Dad's car. Maybe that makes us equal."

"We'll never be equal." Nicky's voice was thick with disgust. "I'm not riding horses so I can damage cars. There must be something really wrong with you. I can see now how you did it. I just can't see why."

Edward laughed, but his voice became thin, creeping. "Horses aren't safe, Gyppo. Watch their eyes. They glow in the dark like devils' eyes. You think you've got a gift with them, but wait till a horse hurts you one day. Then you'll see them for what they really are."

Nicky felt sick. "You're warped in the head, Edward Carter," he whispered. "You should be locked up."

"Think what you like, Gyppo. It's your word against mine. And there's too much against you. Too many reasons why it must have been you."

"Only because you put them there. Only because you set me up. Except – why did you just spray those stupid 'Z's', or 'N's' – why not my full name? You could have dropped me in it a whole lot sooner that way."

Nicky could only see a shadowed outline of Edward's face, but he could feel his eyes burn into him. "Even you wouldn't have been stupid enough to sign your own name. And horses that are tied up don't always stand still—"

"I bet they don't! Especially when they're scared half to death. But I still don't get it – what the hell did you do it *for*?"

"You asked for it. I used to watch you, riding my horse. Making her gallop and jump with your stupid tricks. As if you had some kind of magic power over her. As if you thought you were better than me..." Edward twisted and grappled again, pushing against Nicky, raking his fingernails into his skin.

He had no chance. Nicky's strength, flowing from his anger, was suddenly enormous. He was strong as a giant, pressing into Edward, pinning him down. Edward whimpered, but Nicky didn't let up. He let his mind run backwards through all those night rides with Eclipse. In some of them, at least, Edward must have been out there. Edward must have been watching in the darkness, melting into the shadows as silently as Nicky could do himself. He could guess now at the twisted jealousy that must have wormed its way through Edward, watching Eclipse do for Nicky all the things she would never do with him. And from that mix of jealousy, anger and fear, something almost evil had grown. "Eclipse..." he whispered at last. "You must have hated Eclipse too. You weren't just trying to put her out of action before the jumping trial. You wanted to punish her for all the times you watched her with me..."

Edward swore, a vicious new energy unlocked by Nicky's words. He pushed back at Nicky. Nicky's arms ached. For a moment nothing could be heard but their tight breathing as the two boys battled silently in the darkness.

"Let me go now," Edward wheezed suddenly, breathless as an old man. "I've had enough. We'll call it quits."

"Only if you get out of here," Nicky hissed back. "Only if you never go near that horse again."

"Suits me fine. You were right. I hate everything about her. I can't even stand the way she smells."

Nicky released his hold slowly and rolled free. Edward picked himself up.

For a moment they faced each other. "Now get going," Nicky growled. "I want to sort out Eclipse."

Edward moved a step back, but as Nicky turned away he sprang forward again, grabbing him from behind. Nicky swung sideways, but, unbalanced already, his foot twisted outwards. A fierce pain stabbed into his ankle, his leg buckled awkwardly under him, and he fell.

For a moment everything spun. He felt sick and dizzy. He tried to move, but red hot darts seemed to jab through from his knee to his foot.

As he rolled in agony amongst the mud and leaves he was dimly aware of Edward's footsteps running away.

26

"Nicky! Nicky!"
The words reached Nicky through a haze of pain.

Bretta was kneeling in the darkness beside him. "Are you OK?"

Nicky answered her through gritted teeth. "What are you, psychic or something? How come you keep turning up everywhere?"

"I was looking for Eclipse. Then I heard noises, and saw someone run out of here. It looked like Edward at first, but whoever it was ran off like a wild thing, so it couldn't have been. Liam and Matt have gone chasing after them."

Nicky groaned. "Liam and Matt? That's all I need – Edward's hyenas moving in for the final kill."

"They're here because they were helping me. Dad dropped me off earlier so I could sort out Eclipse. When she wasn't in her usual stable I checked the whole yard. That was when I saw it — the garage door left wide open, and Declan Carter's car missing. I hammered on Liam's door, and they rang the police…" Bretta pulled off her jacket as she talked, and draped it like a blanket over Nicky's leg. "Then I got a really bad feeling about Eclipse. I suppose I was just jumpy because of the car being taken. Matt said Edward had got him to put her out earlier, but I was still getting in a tizz, so they came out here with me…"

Just then there were footsteps, and Liam and Matt crashed their way into the copse. "He got away in Declan Carter's car, I'm sure of it. I'd know that engine growl anywhere," panted Liam.

He shone the torch on to Bretta, noticing Nicky for the first time. His voice hardened. "What are you doing here?"

"The same as you lot. Looking for Eclipse. Or that was the plan, until I met Edward."

"Edward?" Matt appeared, shining his own torch beam full into Nicky's face. "I didn't know he was about. Liam said he'd gone out. Were you fighting?"

"We weren't playing tiddlywinks." Nicky tried to sit up, and winced.

"So where is he now? Is he OK?"

Nicky gave a harsh laugh, the pain still biting into his leg. "He's fine. Made a quick getaway in a stolen car, from what I can make out."

"What do you mean?"

"Your precious Edward. It's him that took his dad's car. And there's nothing wrong with his leg. There probably hasn't been for a long time. He just used it to try and get out of riding."

There was a long silence.

"But why?" said Bretta at last.

"Same reason he's been out driving it lots of other times. So he can get at the horses. Tie them up and spray them."

"You think *Edward's* been doing it?" Bretta's voice was small with horror.

"I know he has. I came out here for the same reason you did, because I was worried about Eclipse, and I caught him. He's got a grudge against horses, and he's got a grudge against Eclipse. He's dangerous."

"I still don't see why…" Bretta faltered, hurt and confused.

"Lots of reasons. Fear of horses. Fear of his dad. Fear of that Olympic team stuff. And luckily for him, he even found a Gyppo to pin it on." Nicky didn't mention the jealousy – the raw hatred he'd heard in Edward's voice earlier. This didn't seem the time to mention his own part in Edward's warped revenge.

"It's a big accusation, Nicky. Can you prove it?" Liam pointed his torch deep into Nicky's eyes, like an interrogator.

Nicky squinted in the glare, but he didn't look away. "I bet if you check your office diary, and then check with the newspapers and stuff, Declan Carter will have been away every time a horse was hurt. That's when Edward used to do it."

There was another silence, then Liam let his hand swing back to his side. "Oh Christ," he swore softly. "I was supposed to keep an eye on him whenever his dad wasn't around, but I never did a proper check on where he went. He usually just said he was going to Billy's or somewhere." He shrugged, and shook his head. "I just took his word for it."

"He did have a thing about that car," Bretta said slowly. She crossed her arms over her chest, as if she was suddenly cold. "He was always in there polishing it and stuff."

"And he never did much with the horses," added Matt. "Not unless his dad was making him."

"That's true," Bretta added. "His dad used to bully him to ride all the time, but he told me once that he hated it. I felt sorry for him. I thought it was because his leg was hurting too much. It was one of the reasons why I wanted to help him. But maybe..."

Nicky was tired of listening to them working it out. He tried to pull himself up, ignoring the jagged pain slicing down from his knee again. "I've got to get to Eclipse now. She's in those bushes. She'll be in a right state." He grabbed a branch to steady himself, but pitched forward, falling awkwardly again. Panting, he leaned back against the trunk of a tree, trying to fight new waves of sickness.

"Don't worry, I'll deal with the horse." Liam waved the torch until it picked out Eclipse, hunched a long way back in the shadows.

She wasn't moving, but as Nicky looked at her, he could see the fear rising in purples and reds all across her body. Her head was turned away, and Nicky realized she'd been keeping still, trying to be invisible, hoping they'd leave her alone. She was locked in a nightmare – sixty million years of instinct screaming at her to run, and nowhere she could go.

Liam stepped nearer, his torch freezing her in its spotlight. Eclipse jerked her head up, snorting. She tried to back away.

"Careful," warned Nicky. "She's pretty scared."

"She knows me," Liam called back over his shoulder. "She'll be fine."

Nicky saw her stiffen. Her eyes rolled in wild panic. She struggled to escape, dry leaves and sticks cracking under her as she twisted away. She'd hurt herself in a minute...

Liam was right up close, his hand stretching out to touch her. Suddenly Nicky saw her shadowy shape rear up, boxing the air with her front legs. Liam dived sideways, and Eclipse's hooves hit the ground with a thud, right where Liam had been standing.

"It's hopeless. I can't get near her."

"Shall I try?" Matt's voice was shaky, and he didn't move forward.

"We can't leave her like that," said Bretta anxiously. "She could break a leg if she struggles any more. I'll see how close I can get."

As Bretta edged forward Eclipse reared again, pressing against spiked brambles that cut and snapped into her. She neighed wildly, a thin scream of terror.

Nicky fought against a new wave of dizziness. He had to pull himself together. Bretta was right. Any minute now Eclipse could fall. He just had to get on with it. He struggled up again, catching at branches to stop himself swaying. "I'll do it," he said. "She won't be scared of me."

"Please, Nicky, leave her. You're hurt already. You won't—"

Nicky ignored Bretta, shook off Liam as he grabbed at his arm, and moved slowly towards Eclipse.

It was agony to walk, but Nicky tried to stay

steady. Any sudden movement might send Eclipse rearing backwards, and even his limp could make him seem strange to her.

Very quietly, he gave her the deep, throaty greeting. Her ears flicked forward and back. She snorted anxiously. The sound was right, and the smell was right, but Nicky was different in a way that confused and frightened her.

Nicky breathed slowly. He had to clear his mind, just concentrate on Eclipse. Otherwise he would only pass his own fear and pain on to her.

He took a step sideways, as if he was walking past, letting her know that he wasn't any threat. But all the time he talked gently, using the soft Gypsy language that he always whispered to her.

Eclipse's ears still flicked, and she was blowing hard, but Nicky knew she was listening. He stopped beside her, still making no eye contact. He was calm now. Calm and in control. He had forgotten his leg. He had forgotten the others. There was only the two of them, him and Eclipse, stood together in the darkness.

Suddenly he felt it. The tension flooded out of her. She knew him. She remembered him. The colours – and the fear – were gone.

Only then did he turn towards her, moving very close, their faces touching. "You'll be OK," he whispered. "I won't let you be scared any more." He rubbed the half-star between her eyes. She stood quietly.

After a moment she nuzzled her nose against him, licking and chewing, then dropped her head low to the ground. It was the action Nicky had been waiting for. Eclipse was saying she felt safe at last. She was ready to stay with him.

"OK, Bretta." Nicky didn't move from Eclipse, and he didn't alter his tone. "Move up close and get rid of the string. She'll be fine now."

Bretta hesitated. "Are you sure it's OK?"

"Trust me."

There was a moment's silence, then Bretta took Matt's penknife and, walking softly forwards, she dropped beneath Eclipse's belly and cut.

Eclipse went on nudging and nuzzling Nicky as if she didn't even notice.

"So what now?" whispered Bretta, drawing close to Nicky.

"I want to ride her back to the stables," he said softly, "but I'll need you to give me a leg up. It has to be you. She's comfortable with you. The others might panic her again."

Slowly Nicky edged his way along Eclipse's side, stroking and rubbing all the time. Then, as the biting pain tore back through his leg, he let Bretta help him on. Eclipse stayed calm and still, and didn't even flinch.

Liam gave a low whistle. "Neat stuff."

Matt fell into step beside him as Nicky rode Eclipse gently out from the bushes. "Liam's right. That was ace. I thought we were going to lose her. I thought she'd mess herself up and have to be shot."

Nicky caught Bretta's eye in the darkness, and grinned suddenly. "Not bad for a Gyppo, eh?"

27

There was a police car waiting when they reached the yard.

Nicky recognized Inspector Whymark as he got out and hurried towards them. "I'm looking for Liam Frazer."

"That's me."

"We've found the car, and we've got the kid that did it back at the station. He was racing down the lane like the devil was chasing him. A danger to himself and everyone else. Now we need to get in touch with Declan Carter. It's a matter of some urgency."

"I've got his mobile number in the office. I'll get it."

As Liam disappeared with Inspector Whymark,

Matt gave a low whistle. "Declan Carter is *not* going to be happy. I wouldn't want to be in Edward's shoes."

"And it's not going to be just the car, is it?" Bretta said quietly. "We're going to have to tell the police about the other stuff. About what he's been doing to horses."

Nicky pressed his head against Eclipse's cheek, trying to decide. It wasn't his way to talk to the police. It wasn't his way to get involved with the gorgios like that. And he wasn't out for revenge. That wasn't his way either. But Bretta was right. The police had to be told, because Edward had to be stopped.

Limping painfully, he led Eclipse into the warmth of the biggest, most spacious stable, gave her a full check over, then followed Bretta and Matt across the yard to the office.

After they'd given Inspector Whymark their statements, Liam drove Bretta and Nicky home. Matt was staying at the yard. Liam promised Nicky that, between them, they would keep a constant check on Eclipse for the rest of the night. It was the only way he could persuade Nicky to leave her and go home.

They dropped Bretta off first. "I'll be over tomorrow," she said, touching Nicky lightly on the shoulder. "I hope your leg's OK."

"Thanks," said Nicky. "But I'm not so worried about my leg. I'm more worried about what Dad's going to say when I turn up like this."

Bretta gave him a long look. He was scratched, bruised, and splattered with mud. "You'd do well as a scarecrow in the school fancy dress."

"Thanks for the compliment."

Bretta squeezed his arm before climbing out of the car. "Any time," she grinned, then gave a brief wave before hurrying indoors.

"I'll come in with you," said Liam, catching Nicky's expression as they drew up outside Nicky's trailer a few minutes later. "I'll make sure it goes all right."

Dad took one look at Nicky as he limped inside. "This had better be good," he said.

28

The classroom door opened suddenly, followed by the steady *thwmp*, *thwmp*, *thwmp* of rubber tapping the ground.

The whole class looked up as Nicky hobbled through on his crutches.

"Sorry I'm late," he said, meeting Miss Bullock's eye.

Miss Bullock nodded. "Just go and sit down. I'm still sorting a few things out. I haven't done the register yet." Her expression was as sour as ever, but Nicky noticed she didn't make any spiked comments about letters home or detention this time.

"I've saved you a seat," whispered Bretta, pulling out the chair beside her. "I tried to see you yesterday. Liam found your bike in the bushes and I brought it round, but Sabrina told me your dad had taken you back to hospital. It sounded awful. She said your ankle was too swollen for them to get a proper look on Saturday night."

Nicky nodded. "I had to go back for an X-ray. Dad moaned about all the waiting around, but he was quite good really. We even had baked tatties in the hospital canteen afterwards."

"So what did the hospital say?"

"Broken ankle mainly," Nicky made a face, "and I've pulled some muscles in the back of my leg."

"Does it hurt?"

"No." Nicky glanced at her, then shrugged. "Well, maybe a bit."

"I've got some good news anyway, to cheer you up."

"Go on." Nicky manoeuvred himself awkwardly into the chair, his plastered foot jutting out to the side.

"Declan Carter called round last night."

"I bet that was a treat for you."

"He spoke to my dad mainly, but I listened behind the door. He seemed different. Quieter. He said Edward was going to his mum's – she lives in London apparently – and he said she'd have to sort him out 'professionally'. He didn't seem to want Edward around any more."

"So he wasn't slammed up in the nick then?"

"They must have kept him at the station for a while, before his dad arrived, but it seems they didn't press charges about the car thing because it was a first offence, and because his dad said he would be dealing with it himself."

"And what about the horses? What are the gavvers doing about that?"

"He got cautioned. I think that means they've got him on record now, and they'll be watching him."

Nicky raised his eyebrows. "So he got away with everything really then."

Bretta looked thoughtful. "Well, it won't be that great with his mum. He told me once they didn't get on, and he's hardly ever seen her since she and his dad split up. Maybe that's partly why he's like he is."

"Are you making excuses for him?"

"Not really. Just reasons, I s'pose. And he hasn't really got away with it. His mum doesn't want him. His dad doesn't want him. The police are on to him. And if he ever does it again…"

"Get out the violins. You'll have me sobbing in a minute." Nicky hesitated, then shrugged. "Well, at least there aren't too many horses in London. It won't be so easy for him to get at them even if he wants to."

"But there are plenty of cars. He'll get in bigger and bigger trouble if he doesn't get stopped with those."

"I s'pose it'll be up to him then." It felt odd in a way, chatting with Bretta in class like this. "So what about Eclipse? What happens to her?"

Bretta's face lit up. "I was saving that till last. It's the best bit. After he'd spoken to Dad, Declan Carter came out to me and asked me if I was prepared to carry on working with her, at least until he's sorted things out."

"That's great," Nicky smiled at her. If it couldn't be him riding Eclipse, he would rather it was Bretta than anyone else.

"But there's more," she said. "I told him about you, and asked if you could come over too."

"He'd never agree to that. Not after everything that's happened."

"You're wrong. He was really interested in you. Apparently your dad told him once that you had a gift with horses, and he remembered you. I think Liam and Matt might have put in a good word too."

"So what did he say?"

"He's more than happy for you to come with me. I think he thinks it'll be good for Eclipse. So now you can see her whenever you want, and once your leg's better you'll be able to ride her too."

Nicky's eyes stung suddenly. He looked away out of the window towards the school playing fields, and remembered how many times he'd dreamed of escaping across them in the past. He didn't feel like that today.

"Nicky Ghiselli!"

Nicky turned as Miss Bullock boomed out his name. He was about to get hammered for daydreaming again.

She glanced down at a sheet on her desk. "We're starting our woodworking projects this morning. I've put you down to lead a team with Bretta. One of you can work out the plans, and the other one can take notes. I'll leave you to decide who does what." Miss Bullock beamed him her huge toothy smile before turning away.

29

It was dusk by the time Dad drove Nicky over to the stables.

He leaned on the five-barred gate, watching Bretta lunge Eclipse in the field.

It was a warm evening, the air sweet with April perfume, and soft pink clouds scudding gently across the faded sky.

Eclipse saw Nicky first, and whickered a greeting as she trotted towards him.

Bretta followed. "Hi there. I hoped you'd come."

Nicky grinned. "Try and keep me away."

Bretta opened the gate, and Nicky hobbled in. He stood close to Eclipse for a moment, leaning against her, his hands stroking the dark silk of her coat. "Get on," he said suddenly.

"But she's not tacked up…"

"She'll be OK. Trust me." Nicky unhooked the lunge rein.

Bretta scrambled up on the gate, and on to Eclipse.

"Walk her round." Nicky limped beside them for a moment. "I'll teach you a few Gypsy secrets."

Then he stood and watched, talking softly, as Bretta and Eclipse walked, then trotted, then cantered around him.

"That was great," Bretta smiled, riding back to him at last. "I can't wait till your leg's better and you can start riding her too."

Nicky hesitated for only a moment. "Stay still," he said, "and budge over."

"What are you doing?"

"I'm getting on," Nicky winked at her suddenly. "You didn't really think a bad leg would stop *me* from riding, did you?" He let go of the crutches, and they dropped with a soft clatter on to the grass. Putting his hands on Eclipse's back, he pulled himself up, ignoring the sharp jabs of protest that raced from his knee to his ankle.

Then, clicking his tongue and squeezing with his good leg, he urged Eclipse forward.

The three of them cantered smoothly across the darkening field, while the full moon rose upwards from behind the clouds.

Don't miss the next title
in the series:

Horse
Healer
Puzzle

1

"That's the oddest-looking horse I've ever seen." Nicky leaned on the gate, watching as the owner slipped a halter on to a gawky brown and white cob, and led him across.

Close up, the horse looked stranger than ever. His head seemed too big. His neck seemed too long. He had a patchy coat – odd brown splodges like pieces from a jigsaw puzzle amongst the white. Some of the colour seemed to trickle down under his belly and inside his legs, as if someone had thrown a can of paint at him. On his face, just over one side, ran a white mark that covered his left eye, then spread all the way down to his mouth. It gave him a lopsided, slightly confused expression.

Nicky unlatched the gate and swung it open for

Tom, the head groom at Mill Farm Riding School, and they walked through together, towards the horse.

"He looks like something from another planet. He'll frighten all the kids in the riding lessons on Saturday mornings. I don't think…" Tom began to joke, then broke off as a fit of coughing suddenly hacked through him. As the cough died, he bent stiffly, running his knotty, weathered hands over the horse's legs.

Nicky was standing at the front of the horse, rubbing his hand gently across the mottled brown fur on its forehead. The horse stood very still, watching him with dark, liquid eyes, the colour rich and warm like melted black chocolate. The eyes had a brightness – almost as if there was a light behind them – that seemed to shine through.

"He's very willing," the owner was saying. "You won't have any trouble with him." He gave a sharp jerk to the nose band, as if to prove that this was a horse who could take a bit of roughness. He wasn't a cruel man, but he was a dealer. He bought and sold horses, and he liked to sell them on quickly. This one was proving harder to shift than most.

Tom walked slowly all round the horse, checking him over. The horse sniffed him back, nuzzling in his pockets and suddenly pulling out a packet of peppermints with his teeth. Tom laughed, and gave him one. "He seems gentle enough. And he looks very fit. If I was buying him with my own money, his looks wouldn't be a problem, but we're not supposed to be pleasing ourselves here. What do you think, Nicky?"

Nicky's green eyes rested on Tom for a moment. He hesitated. He liked this horse, he had a good feeling about it, but he had to be careful too. This was the first time Tom had asked him to come out when he was buying a new horse. He knew Tom would respect his decision, but there was someone back at the yard who would be quick to criticize. "I need to try him. See how he goes."

The owner nodded. "I'll get the tack."

"Don't bother. I'll take him bareback. I won't need long."

Nicky sprang lightly on to the horse, then nudged him gently. The horse flickered his ears and stepped forward. He wasn't a comfortable ride. There was a stiffness about his movements that made him jerky. Nicky pressed him into a trot, and then a canter. The awkwardness was still there. Tom was right. With his odd looks and his uneven stride, he wouldn't be popular with the kids, and that was what they had to think about.

He walked the horse back to where the others were standing and slid off. Immediately the horse turned its head towards him and rubbed its nose against his arm. Nicky ran his fingers through the scraggy mane.

"What d'you think now?" Tom was coughing again. He looked tired suddenly, as if even trying to make a decision was hard work.

Nicky ran his hands through his dark hair and shook his head. The horse wouldn't do. Not for what they were looking for, at any rate. But just then, he caught the horse's eye again. It still held that same warm, liquid beauty, but this time the look seemed empty. Almost resigned. It was as if the light had gone out. Nicky didn't let himself think any more. He just said what he felt, the words almost tumbling out of him. "I think he's great. There's something about him. I think we should have him."

Within ten minutes the gawky skewbald cob was following Nicky quietly into the horse box, and Tom drove them back home to the yard.